A few seconds later a helicopter marked NPS appeared.

The helicopter hovered several hundred feet above, and we saw a guy wearing a Park Service uniform, goggles, and an orange helmet lean out of the passenger window and take a good look at us.

Then he dropped something out of his window, right into camp.

It was a bag of rice, with a note inside. The note read, "63,000 RELEASED THIS MORNING. CAMP HIGH. BE CAREFUL."

"Holy cow," Rita said. "Is this a joke or something?"

Troy muttered grimly, "They didn't look very much like comedians."

"Look," Pug said, pointing at the beach where we'd tied up the boats. The boats were floating fifteen feet offshore. We looked around at each other, and not a word further was spoken, not even a curse. Our fear was rising as fast as the water.

RIVER THUNDER

WILL HOBBS

Published by
Bantam Doubleday Dell Books for Young Readers
a division of
Random House, Inc.
1540 Broadway
New York, New York 10036

Visit us on the Web! www.randomhouse.com

Educators and librarians, for a variety of teaching tools, visit us at www.randomhouse.com/teachers

ISBN: 0-440-22681-3

RL: 6.0

Reprinted by arrangement with Delacorte Press

Printed in the United States of America

March 1999

10 9 8 7 6 5 4 3 2 1

WCD

to Jean

who hears the wren around the bend
and always wants to go again

Chapter

1

"We're here, Jessie! Can you believe it?"

We drove down a steep grade, rounded a corner, and suddenly there it was, my river of dreams, coursing through the desert like a streaming emerald jewel.

It was almost too good to be true. Tomorrow we'd rig rafts and start once more down the Colorado River.

Down Marble Canyon and into the Grand Canyon.

Star and I had the windows rolled down. Our hair was flying and our spirits soaring as we pulled into the parking lot in the asphalt-melting heat of early June.

"We're actually back at Lee's Ferry, Jessie."

"I know," I replied, already buzzing with adrenaline. "And this time, Star, the trip's gonna be *legal*."

The launch ramp immediately below the lot was a mob scene. People were milling around, trucks were unloading mountains of gear, and guides for the river companies were handing life jackets to tourists as they stepped from buses. Star and I got out of the car, stretched, and started looking for Al and Adam, or a van that said DISCOVERY UNLIMITED.

1

I realized more than a little sheepishly that we might be looking for the same van we'd "borrowed" last October. Meeting up with Al, the owner of Discovery Unlimited, was going to be a little strange. We ditched out on him last time, when he was getting ready to take us on the San Juan River, and we pirated the Grand Canyon with his rafts instead.

Hearing from Al had been a complete surprise to Star and me, especially when we realized he was inviting us to come along on his counselors' training trip down the Grand Canyon. His letter explained that we'd be interns, some kind of resource people for the new counselors, just for this one trip. We weren't exactly sure what being interns meant, but we knew we wanted to go.

And one of our old cohorts was going to be with us! Adam had somehow talked Al into hiring him onto his regular summer staff, so it would be the three of us back together again.

Meeting up with Adam was going to be delicious—we knew that Al hadn't told him we were coming. In the letter, Al said to keep it a surprise. We kept scanning the parking lot and the ramp. "Where's our redheaded Ninja?" Star muttered impatiently.

Right then we heard our names shouted and looked to see, emerging from the mob scene, not Adam and Al, but a guy and a girl who were familiar yet not instantly recognizable.

Star and I did a simultaneous double take. Sure enough, it was Rita and Pug, the Thief of Brooklyn and the Big Fella. They were running toward us.

Rita, hyper as ever, was outrunning Pug. I realized what was different about her—her dark hair was cut short and bouncy. Pug looked different too: leaner, older. He was wearing a green baseball cap with the word CASE on it. He had a huge smile on his face, as if Rita and Star and I were his long-lost best friends. I was thinking, What in the world is *he* doing here? Does he think we all have amnesia?

"Holy cow!" Rita hollered. "I don't believe this."

It was so good to hear Rita's New York accent, even to have her face practically in mine. But I was short-circuited by the thought that Al had invited her and Pug, in addition to Star and me, to join his counselors for their training trip.

Especially Pug.

The Big Fella was pointing at our rear fender. "I like your bumper stickers."

On the spot, I should have said that I couldn't believe we were even having this conversation. Had Pug forgotten that we'd split into two camps last time, and that he and his partner Troy were on the other side? He seemed genuinely happy to see us. Like a big puppy dog, I thought—all innocence five minutes after leaving a big deposit in the middle of the kitchen floor.

"Guess whose sticker is which," Star invited him.

Pug scratched his two-day whiskers, then took off his baseball cap and ran his hand over his head, about a month grown out from a crew cut. "Let's see . . . ," he began slowly. " 'PRACTICE RANDOM ACTS OF KINDNESS AND SENSELESS ACTS OF BEAUTY'—that would have to be you, Star. And 'VISUALIZE WHIRLED PEAS'—well, that's Jessie!"

"I coulda told you that in a second," Rita blurted out impatiently. "Hey, guys, I'm still trying to figure this

3

out. Pug didn't know I was going to be here, I didn't know he was, and now you guys show up in this beat-up old VW—"

"It's not beat-up," I objected, "it's a classic. They don't even make these anymore."

Rita threw her head back and laughed, then gave the tire a kick and proclaimed, "Piece of junk!"

Star acted hurt. "Hey, that's Ladybug! You'll hurt her feelings." Star's crescent moon and star earrings jingled musically below her double-pierced ears.

"So you two arrived together somehow—where from?"

"From Colorado," I explained. "Star went home to Boulder with me after the Grand Canyon."

"You're kiddin'. This is like a storybook or something. Star, you were like, homeless, right? Abandoned at some church shelter? Living on the streets?"

I was getting such a kick out of seeing Rita again. She always did have a way of getting right to the point.

Star reached out her arm and hugged me. "Not anymore!"

I said, "Not only that, my dad and my stepmom adopted her. It's all legal and everything. Meet my sister."

"Rhaat onnn!" Pug thundered.

"You're looking lean and mean," I said to Pug. "You must've lost twenty pounds."

The Big Fella was beaming. "Yes, ma'am. Twenty-five pounds. At boot camp, near Tulsa."

"Boot camp!"

"Yes, ma'am, been to hell and lived to tell. It was a cross between prison and basic training. Got out six

4

weeks ago. Been working for a landscaper since then—keeps me in shape."

"Enough!" Rita objected. "Hey, guys, we're fryin' our brains out here. It's a hundred-and-something, you know. Grab your suits—let's go jump in the river!"

We changed in the bathrooms, then ran down the ramp together, weaving our way through all the people and equipment. Rita led us to the river at a gap between a long line of rowed rafts and the gigantic pontoon rafts with motors. The rowed rafts, in comparison, looked like toys.

The Colorado was higher than I remembered, but with the river as wide as it was here, it didn't seem menacing. I did a quick mental calculation to try to guess the effect of more water in the big rapids. They'd be tougher, I imagined, but I didn't give it much thought since I wasn't going to be rowing. It was probably unrealistic to keep hoping I'd get even a few minutes on the oars now and again.

Rita bellied into the river and the rest of us followed. I wasn't prepared for the utter shock of the freezing green water, but instantly I remembered it was coming out of the bottom of Lake Powell, the immense reservoir behind Glen Canyon Dam, which was only fifteen miles upstream. I came up gasping and screaming with the rest of them, and we headed for the nearest shade, a cluster of feathery scrub trees called tamarisks, at the downstream end of the launch ramp.

It was time to figure out what was going on here.

Chapter

2

"Keep your eye out for Al," Rita ordered. "If I'm gonna cook for sixteen people, I want to see what kind of menus he's got."

"Is that what he signed you on for?" I asked. I was thinking, I hope Al and his counselors are partial to garlic, *lots* of garlic.

"Head cook, that's me. Fortunately I had just enough savings for the airline ticket and the bus from Flagstaff—I've been working at Pizza Hut evenings and weekends all year. Al said everything would be covered once I got here."

"I came up short," Pug told us. "I had to beg some cash from my mother. She knew how much this meant to me."

Rita had her beady eyes on me like a cat ready to pounce. "So where'd you get your gas money, Jessie? Your dad's a rich professor, right?"

"Professors aren't rich," I protested. "They hardly make more than high-school teachers. Besides, we had our own gas money. Star's got a job at a nursing home, and she's been selling some of her beadwork jewelry, too; I've been serving up cappuccinos and lattes at a bookstore espresso stand in Boulder."

"Espresso stand . . . sounds pretty upscale to me. Hey, Big Fella, what did Al sign you on for?"

"Said they needed a big, strong guy."

I had the vague feeling that something didn't compute, but it passed.

"Probably they needed a head case," Rita quipped. "Check out his hat."

Pug took it off, twirled it around his finger. " 'Case' makes backhoes, Rita. Ever heard of backhoes?"

"Heard of garden hoes, ladies' hose . . ."

Just then two of the big motor rigs started down the river with fifteen or more passengers on a raft. Everyone was cheering. As we watched them pass, we started to compare notes on the letters we'd gotten from Al. Al wrote each of us that Discovery Unlimited had one permit for a two-week trip in the Grand Canyon, and that he was going to use it to help train his counselors, including Adam. He told each of us that he wanted to give his new counselors the benefit of our experiences on the infamous River Pirates trip.

The thing was, we'd each thought we were the only ones being invited, like we'd been especially chosen. We were all puzzled why Al didn't say in his letters that he was inviting more of us back.

"Maybe it was because it was all on such short notice," I suggested. "He didn't know if anybody could really come, and he didn't want us to get our hopes up for a reunion."

7

Pug had a mischievous grin on his face. "Maybe he thought we'd start plotting against him."

Rita threw him an elbow. "Don't even think about it! If we do good, we might get real jobs. Anyway, my letter said Al was going to be away from base camp until the Grand Canyon trip—just leave a message on his answering machine if I could come. And don't tell Adam, it said. Al wanted to surprise him. I guess we never knew old Al was such a fun-loving guy."

"Not the way I remember it," Pug observed with a smirk.

A cluster of six rowed rafts was starting down the river, three passengers per raft. I was thrilled to see that one of the rafts was rowed by a woman.

Rita looked at Star and me suddenly. "So what did Al tell you guys he needed *you* for?"

"He wanted us to explain to his counselors what it's like from a kid's point of view in his program."

"That's it? Adam could have done that for him, and he's already hired Adam on for the summer."

"No, there was more to it," I admitted. I was squirming. This was going to be embarrassing. "It has to do with Troy."

"Oh, *him*," Rita snapped. "I noticed nobody mentioned his name before this."

"Al said he realized that ditching out on Discovery Unlimited was Troy's idea in the first place, but that all of us bought into the 'alternate reality' that Troy created. He wants us to teach his counselors . . . let's see if I can remember how he put this . . . 'how Troy was able to unite us as adversaries to the program, especially the girls.' "

"I see what he's getting at. I remember the way Troy would stare at everybody, especially you, with his baby blues."

"Don't remind me," I groaned. "He had us all around his finger at one time or another."

Pug came to my defense. "I know what Jessie felt like. I woulda marched into hell if Troy told me to."

"This is a crock," Rita said. "Jessie shouldn't have to tell girl stuff to Al's counselors. What's so new about any of it, anyhow? Cute guy pulls cute chick's chain—end of story."

I reddened, and not from the heat.

Rita waved her arm dismissively. "I say, let's go down the river and have a blast. Who wants to keep talking about Troy? He was just a spoiled rich kid on a power trip."

"Amen," I agreed.

"Hey, but what about Freddy?" Rita exclaimed. "The way everybody's showing up, shouldn't we be looking around for him, too? Now, if Al needed somebody to teach his counselors a thing or two about the wilderness, Freddy would be the one."

"I can answer that," Star piped up. "Jessie and I got a card from Freddy this spring. He got into a training program up in Montana for fighting big forest fires. He's going to be a Hotshot for the Forest Service."

"I'd love to see him," I added, "but I can't picture him giving up the Hotshots. That was his dream."

Rita sprang to her feet, full of nervous energy. "So where are those guys? In the letter, it said 'Be there by five for dinner.' It's five."

While we were talking, we'd seen almost all the rafts

9

launch and start down the river. We got up and walked over to a rowed raft that said RIVER RANGER along the side. No one was around, so I got in and sat on the ranger's seat and tried my hands on the oars.

"You coulda rowed Upset," Rita declared.

"I'd like to think so," I said. I was a little surprised she remembered. Just when I was primed to row my first big rapid, they'd caught us. Having committed, and then suddenly losing the chance to row a piece of really big water . . . it left me in limbo. All winter long, back at home, I was rowing whitewater in my sleep, dealing with crashing waves, rocks, and bottomless holes. The dreams would go on for hours. Sometimes I'd go to school the next day exhausted from "virtual rowing."

The river had stayed with me every day since we'd been caught and flown out. At home, in school, skiing, training on my mountain bike—there wasn't a day went by that I hadn't flashed on the Canyon. There was so much more to it than the whitewater, which was amazing enough. I kept remembering the vastness, the changing light, the cascading song of the canyon wren. The Grand Canyon had seeped into my soul.

We took another plunge in the river. Streaming water, we started up the ramp. Just then I spotted him—a guy getting out of a new Land Rover. He was tall and blond, long-legged, buffed, totally tanned. This guy was a real styler: sunglasses, muscle T-shirt, running shorts, river sandals.

"Wait a minute," I said. "That's Troy."

Chapter

3

Rita had her hands on her hips. "Give me a break! Al invited you?"

Troy held his arms out wide, palms up, and gave us his trademark winning smile. His bluer-than-blue eyes made the rounds, asking . . . for what? When they came to mine, there was a moment of complicated, hypercharged emotion that ran between us like a fiber-optic cable carrying a thousand messages at once. It was the worst kind of electricity.

"Hi, Rita," Troy said warmly. "Hi, Star; hi, Big Fella." And then, a little delayed, his eyes returned to mine. "Hi, Jessie."

His voice sounded gentle, maybe even endearing, but I knew he must hate me. I'd left him on the shore—we'd all left him. This was going to complicate everything, maybe unbearably. How could Al have invited him?

Troy had a tiny diamond stud in his left earlobe. It was so Troy-like, it made me wonder if he'd had it before, but I realized it was new.

Nobody spoke, and then Troy said lightly, with his

familiar, laid-back delivery, "You all look a little different."

I was wondering if that was true of me. Hair still shoulder-length, still brown. Eyes still brown. Same height, same weight. Maybe I was stronger, that's all. "You're looking good, everybody," he continued, a little off-balance.

Everybody was staring at him. He was still Troy, still a heavy, that much was obvious.

Troy grinned, kept trying. "Rita, I like your hair."

Rita groaned, and turned to the rest of us. "Pinch me. I must be trapped in some kind of 'alternate reality.' "

Troy acted like Rita was a mosquito whose buzzing was barely noticeable. "Star, I'm glad to see you're still wearing that lucky crystal around your neck. All you guys look great . . . I really mean it. I'm happy to be here. Look where we are."

No one moved.

"I'm hungry," Pug declared as he reached to kick a small rock across the asphalt. "Where are those guys?"

I realized Pug was just as baffled and deflated as the rest of us.

"Let's drive up to the café at the trading post," Troy said to him and all of us. "That's the only place to eat around here, anyway. Al will look for us there."

"Talked me into it," Pug said, heading toward Troy's Land Rover.

At Marble Canyon Trading Post we entered through a combination gift shop, grocery, and river supply, where Pug paused to stare at enormous trout mounted on the walls. We passed into a large, pine-paneled dining room

12

surrounded by photographs of all manner of river mayhem. I walked up to one picture that was poster-sized, a close-up of one of those giant motor rafts in a rapid of monstrous proportions. It was in the act of flipping.

Star was at my side, eyes wide as mine. The photo caught fifteen or twenty people going airborne into churning red water as the pontoon raft was standing on one side and starting to go over.

"Way to the ugly," jested a voice over my shoulder. It was Troy, casual as ever.

"What rapid is that?" I asked the waitress passing by.

"Lava Falls. That's a thirty-seven-foot motor rig you're looking at, in Lava Falls."

"Oh," I said to Star. "No wonder we didn't recognize it. We never got to Lava."

Rita had joined us, and heard the name of the rapid. She crunched up her face and gave the picture its due. Then she laughed, a sort of "Heh-heh-heh," and said, "We'll kick its butt."

"Now that I'm sick to my stomach," I said, "let's eat."

Most of us ordered burgers and fries. Pug asked for the biggest steak on the menu. "Cooked very rare," he specified, and everybody laughed, including the waitress. It arrived so bloody, Rita remarked that it had probably been alive a few minutes earlier behind the trading post. Star, seated next to Pug and seeming tinier than she really was, kept her eyes fixed on her dinner salad. Star had recently become a vegetarian.

Everyone kept an eye on the pass-through from the gift shop, expecting Al and Adam to show up. Everyone

13

except for Troy, who seemed more intent on catching my gaze and having some kind of nonverbal heart-to-heart. What was it he wanted to say?

We kept waiting, ordered dessert and coffee, waited some more. I was getting nervous overhearing bits of conversation from some people three tables away who kept talking about "the high water." I caught the names of some of the rapids—Hance, Crystal, Lava, and more.

The names of the rapids were spoken with awe, and with nervousness that sounded much stronger than an undercurrent. Dread, that's what it sounded like to me. The sick-to-my-stomach sensation of being about to run one of those Big Drops returned all too vividly to mind, and I set aside my apple pie à la mode after only a few bites. At least we were going to be under the protection of Discovery Unlimited. Hang on and enjoy the ride!

Seven o'clock rolled around. Suddenly Rita said, "I got it!" Her dark eyes were big and her eyebrows suggested wide-bladed, curving swords. "Al's not coming," she said decisively.

"Whaddaya mean he's not coming?" Pug protested.

"Listen. Al never got mad enough at us, which I always thought was suspicious. This is all a joke he's playing on us, for revenge."

"I still don't get it," Pug insisted. "What's the joke?"

Rita went bug-eyed and stared across the table at him. "Al's not coming, that's what I'm getting at, Pug. No rafts tomorrow, no trip. We all go home, ha-ha."

Pug looked quickly around the table to see what the rest of us thought. I wondered if it could be true. After a second I knew it couldn't be. "Al could get into trouble for doing something like that—maybe even get sued.

You can't be in business and do something that unprofessional. I still think he's coming."

"I'm afraid I have the answer," Troy said, wiping his mouth with his napkin and replacing it neatly beside his plate. Troy was seated at the head of the table—because nobody wanted to sit beside him? Or had he assumed it was his rightful position? He leaned back in his chair, tilting onto the back legs, yawned, and joined his hands behind his head, elbows out in the air.

Rita said, "Are you doing some kind of yoga or something, Troy? Out with your theory. Let's hear it."

Troy eased the chair down and folded his hands in his lap. "Well, Al's not coming, like you said."

"All you have to say is ditto?"

Troy put his head down for a second. When he looked up, his face had the most awkward expression I'd ever seen on it. Then he said, "I'm Al."

I was completely confused. So was everyone.

Rita reacted by slamming her open hand on the table. The noise startled us all, including Troy. People in the café were looking at us. Rita didn't care. She pointed her finger at Troy. "I'm not taking anything off anybody, Troy, especially you. So cut the weirdness. Al is a Vietnam vet who runs an outdoor school for messed-up kids. And you're not him."

Troy said evenly, "What I'm trying to say is, it was me who wrote those letters to you guys."

Pug made no effort to disguise his confusion. "Say what? You did what?"

Star and I had our jaws on the floor. "You did what?" we echoed.

"I wrote the letters."

15

Troy looked at each of us, his piercing blue eyes going around like a searchlight. "I had something to offer you," he explained, "but if I'd come right out with it, you wouldn't be here now. You would've turned me down or your parents would've turned me down."

"Turn what down?" insisted Star. Star was not as passive as Troy might have remembered her. "Tell us the truth now, Troy. Whatever it is you're about to tell us, tell us the truth for once."

"I will," he promised. "Listen. Just hear me out. I turned eighteen around Christmas—"

"Bravo!" Rita cheered, but when Pug gave her a pained look, and turned back to Troy, Rita held her tongue. Troy proceeded to tell us how he had obtained a private permit to run the Grand Canyon. He'd applied, all nice and legal, then phoned in half a dozen times a day for months to ask if there were any cancellations. And wouldn't you know, he got one. A trip canceled and he got their date. "I got a private permit for tomorrow, the fourth of June," he concluded. "That's our lucky date. We're totally legal. Doesn't matter a bit if some of us are under eighteen, either."

"I don't believe this," I said.

"And what are we going to use for rafts?" Rita demanded. "Did you suddenly inherit a full line of rafting equipment?"

"That part was simple," he explained. "I've hired a raft rental company out of Flagstaff to completely outfit our trip. They even cater the food. They just drop everything off and we jump on and go. The whole trip is on me, folks."

16

"What for . . . why would you . . . ?" Rita was sputtering.

"Hey, what about Adam?" Pug remembered. "Is he coming or not?"

"I wish. No way I could've asked him—he really *is* working for Al this summer."

"That would've blown Troy's cover," Rita explained, putting the pieces together. "What about the letterhead, Troy? It looked real legitimate. Man, you've got a lot of nerve. How'd you do that?"

"That was easy. I had some of Al's old stationery. Any print shop could do that. Of course, I had to change the phone number and set up a new one through an answering service in Colorado. I was just hoping none of you would dig up the number from the actual letterhead, or write Al or Adam. It's not like this was all foolproof or anything. . . ."

I was so steamed. "Obviously not," I said. "You got four fools right here who answered your beck and call."

"I knew you'd thank me in the end," he explained, a grin playing on his lips.

I couldn't take his arrogance. "Right, Troy. After you've played God with our lives, we're just going to jump on your rented boats and go down the Grand Canyon with you."

He held up his hand. "Just hear me out before you say anything more. Just a little longer."

"Five more minutes and get to the point," I said. I felt myself starting to get *really* angry.

"More than anything, I've been wanting to get back to the Canyon. Last October, that was hands down the

17

greatest time I've ever had in my life, before I spoiled it—"

"Get this," Rita interrupted. "I think we're about to get an apology."

"I mean it," he implored. "Being with you guys, rowing a raft on big water—it was the greatest thing in the world. Think about this: I could've paid my way on any commercial trip. But having someone else take you down the Canyon instead of doing it yourself, it just couldn't compare. You know that. It couldn't come close. That's why I looked into getting a private permit. You have to wait six or seven years, or you can try and score a cancellation. I worked hard at it, and have the phone bill to show for it. I was amazed when I got one."

I met his eyes. "So that's when you started thinking about scamming us."

"Look, Jessie," he pleaded. "I spoiled it last time. I know that. I want to make it up to you, all of you—I really do. I can't blame you for not trusting me, but there's no one else I'd want to go with except you guys."

Rita started applauding. "First place in the dramatic category for leading man goes to . . . Troy. That was touching."

He put his hands on the table. "Look. Every one of you answered the call. It was because of the Canyon. You all want to get back, same as me. I figured, if I could just get you here, and you could see that you had another chance to run the Canyon—well, you just couldn't turn it down, no matter how you felt about me."

I was shaking my head. "You have to be the greatest

manipulator of all time. You mustn't think very highly of us, to think we could be bought so easily."

"Let's get *past* that, Jessie," he implored. "Let's get *beyond* that."

Rita was beside herself. "That's a good one, Troy. That must be how they talk out in L.A."

"Troy," I said, "you lied to us. This whole setup is a lie. Why should we trust you? You can't repair broken friendships with money."

He started to get up. His pride was badly wounded.

"I don't know what you expected," I snapped at him.

"Look," he insisted. "Everybody's capable of changing for the better. Even me. Think about it. You don't have to make up your minds tonight. If you don't want to go in the morning, we won't go. I gave it my best shot. I'll reimburse your travel money."

Rita had an ironic smile on her face. "You're a piece of work, Troy."

"I promise everybody this," Troy said, a flash of his old confidence reappearing. "We'll decide everything democratically. It won't be *my* trip. I'm not going to tell anybody what to do, ever."

"Praise be," Rita cracked.

"You can outvote me every time, and as far as the money goes—there's no strings attached."

Suddenly he got real intense. "There's only one thing that's not going to be democratic. . . ."

"What's that?" asked Pug, who was following with utter attention.

"We don't have enough people to paddle a paddle raft, like last time. There's just five of us. With all the gear, it's going to take two boats, and they're both going to be rowed rafts, like the one Jessie and I took turns at last time."

"You mostly rowed it," I reminded him.

"We have to agree before we ever start," he continued, "that I'm rowing one of the rafts all the way down. That's something I want for myself out of this trip. The other part is that Jessie rows the other raft."

Suddenly everybody was looking at me, Troy included, with his tractor-beam eyes.

"Jessie's the one with the experience, and I remember how badly she wanted to row. Even if I ruined it between us, that's something I can do for her—make it possible for her to row a raft all the way through the Grand Canyon. Unless she asks for somebody else to take over, nobody even mentions the possibility. It'll be Jessie's raft."

Chapter

4

Halfway back to the campground at Lee's Ferry, I got panicky. "Slow down, Star," I said, feeling out of breath. "There's a curve coming up. Let them get around it. *Slow down!*"

Star's delicate eyebrows rose in alarm. She quickly geared the Bug down to a creep. Troy's Land Rover disappeared around the corner. "I just realized what we're doing," I said. "We're *following* Troy. This is a big mistake!"

"I see what you mean, Jessie."

"Turn around. Fast, before they catch on!"

Star did a tight U-turn and gunned the Bug back toward the trading post. Looking over my shoulder, I said, "Troy would have just kept working us once we got to the campground."

At the trading post, we turned left. Within a few hundred yards, we were approaching the bridge over Marble Canyon. "Let's just get out of the car," I said.

We sat on a picnic table in the gathering twilight. Bats

were flitting around unpredictably like harbingers of chaos. I said, "I'm so furious I could scream."

"Maybe you should."

I've never been given to histrionics, but that's what I did—I screamed, real loud.

Hearing myself scream made me start laughing. "I feel like an emotional teeter-totter," I said, sniffling. "A complete yo-yo."

"There's probably something to be said for screaming," Star suggested. "You must have needed to flatten out your brain waves."

"I do feel a little better."

We started walking down a little trail that left from the parking lot and wound its way down to the bridge abutments. We sat down below the bridge watching the blending of the twilight colors on the canyon walls and listening to the murmur of the river far below. The Colorado, a metallic blue black, made a bend downstream and disappeared.

"It's just so frustrating," I said. "We thought we were flying along as free as birds, and instead it turns out we're caught in a spiderweb."

"I know," Star said gently. "You thought he was out of your life, didn't you?"

"I wish it was that easy. I'd promised myself I wouldn't talk about him, not even to you. I felt like if I did—if I admitted I was still thinking about him—it would just make things worse."

"I could tell you didn't want me to bring him up, so I didn't."

"All winter and spring, it was as if I was still picking

22

up his signals on my radar screen or something. Can you believe, I even imagined I saw his face in the crowd near the finish of my bike race? I was going so fast toward the bottom of the mountain, everything was a blur, but I really thought I saw him for a second."

"You thought you saw him in Boulder?"

"I know—it says a lot about me. What a stupid thing to pop into my head! He makes me crazy, I guess. What I'd hated about Troy was the way he tried to control me, and yet there I was, back at home, still allowing him to have some influence over me. I don't know why I can't shake him off—maybe it's because we never said good-bye, or bad-bye, or anything at all. No ending, just all of a sudden he was gone."

"Like with my mother, when she took off," Star said softly. "No resolution."

"And now here he is again, asking us to trust him. This is a scam, Star, it's got to be. Troy shows his bright side to the world, but then there's that darker side he tries to keep hidden. I've seen it before, and I don't want any part of it. He must be seriously sick, to go to these lengths."

"Almost desperate," Star suggested thoughtfully.

"Desperate?" I asked. "Troy? I don't think I under-stand." I wasn't sure I wanted to hear what was coming, especially if it was going to be misplaced sympathy.

Star gathered her thoughts. "There was something in his voice, Jessie. Something different. I think he's just so tired of himself. I really heard him when he talked about how people can change. Maybe he's desperate to change his life. Just maybe, he's sincere."

23

My temples were throbbing. "You always think the best of people. But what if that's exactly what he wants us to think? What if we're like fish nibbling at his bait? C'mon, Jessie; C'mon, Star, eat a little more. . . ."

Star answered gently, "The rest of us have changed, Jessie. Think about it. We shouldn't get stuck in the way we look at things—everything's always changing."

"Maybe even Troy?" I said dubiously, to complete her thought.

"Maybe we should consult *The Book of Changes,*" she whispered. "I brought it with me. It's in my daypack."

Star pulled a bundle out of her daypack and opened it carefully. First she spread her blue silk scarf on the slickrock, then lit a small red candle. Next to the candle she set a leather-bound book. From a beaded buckskin pouch she removed three ancient-looking coins and held them loosely in her hand.

Star had found her new oracle, this book of ancient Chinese wisdom, in the bookstore where I worked. It had gradually replaced her timeworn tarot cards. Tossing the coins six times could result in any of sixty-four different readings. The way I'd come to understand it, the reading you threw was supposed to give you insight into dealing with your present situation.

"Are you ready, Jessie?" she asked.

I nodded. With the candlelight flickering on the girders behind her, Star began to throw the coins. She recorded the tallies of heads and tails in a little notebook. Star truly believes that the pattern that results from the six throws isn't accidental. She believes it's a sign, an expression of "synchronicity." Star is very stubborn

24

about not believing in "mere chance." I'm not so sure, but I couldn't see any harm in it.

When she was all done with her calculations, and had turned hopefully to the reading she'd thrown, she looked dismayed. "What is it?" I asked.

" 'DECAY,' " she replied. "I never got this reading before."

"Sounds awful, but appropriate. What else does it say?"

" 'MAKE GOOD AGAIN THAT WHICH HAS BEEN SPOILED.' "

My heart skipped a beat. Troy had even used the word "spoiled." That's what he'd said—"I spoiled it."

"Read it to me," I urged.

"Here goes: 'What has been spoiled as a result of human misdeeds can be restored with healing intention and honest efforts. We must begin anew. We must not shrink from toil and danger."

Every word went pouring through me. Out of sixty-four possible readings, how was it that Star happened to throw this one at this moment?

Quietly Star put the book away. "Jessie, it might be wrong not to let somebody have their chance to make good. 'Make good again that which has been spoiled' works both ways."

"I don't know, Star, I just don't know." Now I was more confused than ever. "Let's sleep on it."

We went back to the car for our ground pads and bags, and slept right there under the bridge. I slept fitfully at best. Maybe I was the only one who could row the other boat, or have half a chance of rowing it, but why did it have to be so much about *me?* Troy said he "wanted to make it up to me." I kept asking myself if that rang true. What did he want from me?

In the morning, I awoke to the song of the canyon wren, that delicate, cascading waterfall of innocence.

Star was still asleep. I slipped out of my bag, went to the edge of the cliff, and sat down. I listened to the sound of the river echoing up the canyon walls. Again and again, like an invitation, came the call of the wren. The morning light was so golden, I just started crying.

Then Star was at my side. She put her arm around my shoulder.

"I'm muddled," I told her. "Totally muddled."

We drove back to the trading post, ate breakfast at the café, and stalled for time. Star let me be. I kept trying to see into Troy's heart. I kept trying to remember everything he'd said at dinner, every nuance of his voice and facial expression. Star's reading from her book had such a hold on me. *"What has been spoiled as a result of human misdeeds can be restored with healing intention and honest efforts."*

I wanted to believe that. My father likes to say that it's up to each of us "to listen to the better angels of our nature." I wondered, Is Troy really trying to do that?

I couldn't call and talk it over with my father. He was in South America with my stepmom, maybe in the rain forest already. He was finally getting the chance to go back and visit the people he'd studied for his dissertation so many years before.

"Let's try to reach Adam," I said to Star. "I want to talk to him about this."

The phone was outside, by the gas station. I asked the

operator for a listing for Discovery Unlimited in Silverton, Colorado. A girl answered; she sounded about my age. She said she'd send somebody to go find him. A few minutes later, it was Adam's voice saying hello.

Adam was flabbergasted. "You're kidding," he kept saying. "Troy did that? He's got a private permit? You'd row the other raft? Pug was in boot camp? Rita made it all the way from New York?"

He kept saying he was blown away, and I'm sure he was.

"But what would *you* do, Adam? Would you do it?"

"Hey, I'm the wrong guy to be asking. You know me . . . the Canyon, are you kidding? You know what I'd do! In fact, it's only a six- or seven-hour drive from here—maybe I should quit right now and come join you! I got a car; I drove out here from Kansas!"

"Don't do that," I said. "That's not why I called."

"I won't, I was just talking. I'm so lucky to be working here, I'd never do something that stupid. Look, Jessie, you have to make your own decision."

"But what about Troy?" I asked. "Would you trust him?"

Adam hesitated. "Personally . . . ? I guess I might give him another chance, but then again, if he weren't dangling the Grand Canyon in front of my nose, I'm not sure I would!"

"Well, thanks, Ninja. I wish we'd stayed in better touch. Give me your prediction, Adam. What am I going to do?"

"Not fair!"

"Tell me, anyway."

"You want to row the Canyon, Jessie."

Chapter

5

Troy was lounging in the boatman's seat on one of the rafts when I got there. He was bare-chested, sipping a soda, flipping through the waterproof mile-by-mile map, keeping his mouth shut. Somehow he sensed that the less said, the better.

The rental company from Flagstaff had already come and gone. Postponing my decision, I let my eyes run over the equipment. The rafts were beautiful, dark gray sixteen-footers with bright yellow bumper stripes around the middle of the tubes, and they were outfitted to perfection. Both rafts even had solar shower bags lashed on the back, to be heated by the sun as we floated downstream. The details were impressive. Every life jacket was equipped with a short-handled knife in a hard plastic scabbard over the chest, where you could get at it in a second in an emergency.

I sat through the ranger's slide show and orientation lecture in the Park Service trailer still thinking I was making up my mind.

The ranger started in with Major John Wesley Powell's historic first run of the Grand Canyon in 1869. As he talked on, telling us all the Park Service rules and regulations, my mind drifted. I was having an imaginary conversation with my father. He was saying, "You're going to be a senior in just a few months, and then you'll be flying the nest." My father had been saying that a lot lately. "I think you should use your own good judgment," he went on. He'd been saying that a lot, too.

What good judgment?

Back at the ramp again, I was in a daze. Even as I was strapping down our dry bags at the back of the raft, I was treating it like a rehearsal. The ramp was crowded with people rigging boats again, and it was hot, much too hot. I kept hearing snatches of conversation about the high water and the big rapids. The gist was, they were going to be worse than usual, especially Crystal and Lava.

There was a rumor going around that the Bureau of Reclamation, or Wreck-the-Nation as some were calling it, had misjudged the rate of the runoff from the snowmelt in the Rockies, and that we'd be looking at flows even higher than the 42,000 cubic feet per second we were looking at right now. I wished I could remember what the numbers were last fall when we'd run the Canyon.

I was getting knee-knocking, stomach-ripping *afraid*.

Teetering with indecision, I looked up and saw Troy right in front of me, his intense blue eyes sympathetic and warm. "Jessie," he said quietly, so no one else could hear. "You really don't have to do this if you don't want to."

He could tell how pitiful I was, I was sure of it. "I

know that," I muttered, and I wondered if he was enjoying this.

Troy stroked his chin and looked away. "It's going to be rough water, from everything I'm hearing. Tougher than last time, if that's possible." Then he looked back at me with undisguised doubt.

Now that it had come down to it, and the Canyon had become a whole lot more real than he remembered, he didn't think I could row it. Maybe he'd staged all of this to prove a point, to exact some kind of petty revenge. I had no idea what he was really thinking.

"I just want you to know," he added earnestly, "it's your decision."

I didn't know if I could row it either, but if somebody's going to tell me I can't do something, I'll break every bone in my body proving them wrong.

With a glance I saw Rita and Pug up in front of Troy's raft, quiet as church mice and all ready to go, trying not to look at me directly. Pug had already stowed the bowline. They both knew the trip was a no-go without me.

Star was calmly sitting on the sand and waiting. I knew she was with me either way. Unfortunately I couldn't share her philosophical acceptance that whatever I decided would work out for the best.

Forget about Troy, I told myself, and his reverse-psychology mind game, if that's what he's playing. This is about me and the Canyon.

I sat down next to Star in the sand, took a long look downstream, took a deep breath. Managing a smile, I said, "We must not shrink from toil and danger."

A few seconds later she was untying the bowline from the steel cable running across the ramp, and I was sitting on the boatman's seat, the padded top of the big cooler. Star was wrapping the rope around her elbow and making a tidy bundle. Now she was tucking it under the chicken line where it ran around the front of the raft.

Star jumped in the raft. I realized she was looking at me as if she was seeing a ghost with oars.

I started pulling for the current. "I'll make a beautiful corpse," I wisecracked.

Star touched the crystal at her neck. "Don't ever say that," she pleaded, and turned to face the oncoming riffles.

Chapter

6

"Calm down," I whispered to myself. "Settle down."
I tucked the oars under my knees so the blades would
stay up in the air, took a long drink of water, looked
around. The cliffs of Marble Canyon were angling up
and out of the earth on both sides. A fisherman waved
from the right, Star waved back. Swallows were knifing
the air above us and skimming the water ahead.

The river was narrowing into a run of whitewater,
which Troy was about to enter. "Paria Riffle," Star announced, reading from our waterproof mile-by-mile
guide. "It's rated as a 1 on the 10-scale."

I pointed the bow of the raft straight down the glassy
green tongue of water that led into the riffle, and rode it
down into the chop of the whitewater. We were soaked
by the tailwaves down at the end, even though I had
maneuvered with the oars to take them head-on.

The water was so cold. "How's that for refreshing?" I
shouted.

Star was reaching for the bail bucket. "That was only
a 1!"

I dug with the oars to pull away from a huge slab of rock sticking out of the river. I kept us off the rock, but in a few seconds the raft was caught in a big boiling eddy that captured us and shot us back upstream.

Pull, I told myself. *Pull!* The raft seemed so heavy. I looked around, trying to figure out where all the weight was coming from. The aluminum rowing frame itself, with the folding table that made the passenger deck across the front, didn't look that heavy. All those metal army boxes full of canned food suspended underneath the deck must be a lot of the weight. When I added in the huge fresh-food cooler I was sitting on and the big tarped load behind me, I began to get the picture. Inside the tarp, we'd stowed our dry bags full of clothes and personal stuff; and underneath them, a twenty-pound propane bottle, two propane stoves and a lantern, even a pickle barrel full of charcoal.

Troy was carrying as much, including the dry-ice frozen cooler he was sitting on and the huge aluminum kitchen box. His army boxes included two that were marked HUMAN WASTE.

We slipped back into the current. Star was distressed over how hard I'd had to work to get out of a little eddy, but she said encouragingly, "Good thing you're in such good shape from skiing and mountain biking."

"I'll get the hang of it," I promised her. "One or two strokes a little earlier and that eddy wouldn't have grabbed us."

I checked my right palm. It already had a sore spot. One mile down, two hundred and twenty-four miles to go. My hands were going to blister badly. I wished I had brought gloves.

33

Within a few minutes the walls of Marble Canyon were several hundred feet high and growing. Up ahead on the left, Troy had pulled out onto a beach of white sand. He was tying up as Rita and Pug were having a footrace down to the lagoon at the far end of the beach.

By the time Star and I touched shore they'd run all the way back, and were panting and laughing. "Lunchtime!" Rita gasped. "But first I need a little hydrotherapy!" She ran off the top of the beach, jumped, and cannonballed into the backwater pool where we'd pulled out.

Pug was looking up and down the sparkling green river, then up the canyon walls to the blue, blue sky, and grinning. Troy was standing back quietly, taking in the four of us and the Canyon. He was pretty pleased with himself. I walked past him, looking for something to tie to. As I walked by, he said, "Back on the river, Jessie!"

For want of anything better to say, I answered, "Here we are."

"I'll get the table off your raft," Troy offered.

Troy? I thought. Troy's going to do it himself?

"Out of my way, everybody!" Rita shouted. Water was still pouring off her bathing suit and she was shaking water out of her short black hair like a wet puppy. "I'm the cook—stand by for orders! Man, if my friends could see me now. They have no conception. *No conception!* Jessie, you weren't sure about doing this trip? Are you crazy?"

"Pretty nice," I said. "We're back."

"Hey, this is a brand-new day in paradise, and it's hot this time! And you should see these menus! Man, you're never going to eat like this in your *life*! Everybody, wash

34

your hands in the big Colorado, like the ranger said, before you even think about getting near this table to help or eat. Like the man said, dysentery is hardly delightful. Soap's in the kitchen box! Go, go!"

Star and I took the shock treatment of full immersion in the river. The T-shirts we'd pulled over our bathing suits would keep us cool as they dried.

"Not over the sand, Troy!" Rita shouted. "The man said wash your hands in the big Colorado, shampoo in the big Colorado, pee in the big Colorado!"

I was curious to see if Troy was going to stand corrected. It didn't come naturally, I remembered. He smiled good-naturedly and recited, " 'Twelve thousand people have to use these beaches every season.' "

Star and I helped to lay out the bread, rye and whole wheat, the cheeses, Swiss and cheddar, the cold cuts, roast beef and turkey. There were tomatoes, lettuce, sprouts, avocados, carrot sticks—Troy's caterers had even anticipated vegetarians—and there were pickles, choices of fresh fruit, chips, and cookies.

"I asked for meals for seven," Troy commented with a touch of his pride showing, "just to make sure we wouldn't starve."

Never one to run from the sight of food, Pug was already building an enormous sandwich while stuffing a handful of potato chips into his mouth. "Feed me and I'll love you forever," he crooned to no one in particular. "I'll get some sodas out of the drag bag. Who needs one?"

"Eat by the river," Rita ordered. "Hey, Star, you shoulda cut your hair short, like mine. Much easier. Maybe I can braid it for you later."

"That's the best way to take care of this hair," Star agreed. "Keep it out of the way."

"Sign me up," Pug joined in, rubbing the half-inch fuzz on his skull. "I can't do a thing with my hair."

Troy was looking like he'd love to join in, but he held back.

Rita tried to encircle Pug's bicep with her hand. Of course her hand didn't reach halfway around. "Go put your shirt on—we're impressed already with your bis and your pecs and your abs. Hey, Big Fella, you're lobstering. What kind of sunscreen you using?"

"Tanning oil," he admitted.

"You can use cooking oil if you run out! Do you as much good!"

Star and I were cracking up, and Troy had his hand over his mouth.

"Who wants to wrestle?" Rita hollered, cookies in both hands. "I'll take all comers. Gotta warn you, though, any illegal holds on this chick and I'll bite your ear off! Feed it to the crocodiles!"

"I'll pass," Troy said.

"Good. Any weirdness out of last year's captain—this year's banker—we'll have both his ears!"

Excellent, Rita reminding Troy of the terms. She has her ways.

"I think Rita's due for some more hydrotherapy," Troy commented playfully. "Pug, should we?"

Pug looked at Troy and seemed to recall they were old buddies. Then he sized up Rita. Rita has a slim build, but she's strong—she has broad shoulders, same as I do. "I'm pretty attached to my ears," Pug said slowly.

From upstream came the sound of a motor, and soon

one of those monster rigs appeared—a huge elongated donut with big torpedo-shaped outrigger pontoons on either side. The boatman, a young guy with a long ponytail, slowed the motor as they came by. The passengers, a dozen or so men, were drinking beer. We could hear everything they were saying. "Look, those are lawn chairs they got tied to the back of their rafts!" "Hey, Bruce, how come we don't have any?" "What do we have we can trade for lawn chairs?" "What do we have we can trade for their women?"

"Bozos!" Rita shouted with her considerable lung power.

Boy, did that get them stirred up. But the boatman gunned his motor, and they were gone. I realized we'd never see them again. Those trips do the Canyon in a week. We weren't taking out until our fourteenth day.

Pug broke out a fishing pole. Star started doing her Tai Chi exercises down on the end of the beach. I stuck close to the raft and did some stretching. On Pug's second cast, a fish struck. "Hookup!" he cried. His pole was bent almost double. Rita, Troy, and I ran to see. "Here, troutie, big troutie," Pug crooned. "Keep him?" he asked Rita anxiously.

"Only one," she ruled. "For hors d'oeuvres. We got prawns for the entrée. I'm already starting to thaw them out."

"As you wish."

I went to studying the mile-by-mile guide. The first rapid to come up would be Badger Creek Rapid at Mile 8. It was rated a 5 at high water, which was listed as anything over 35,000 cubic feet per second.

"Mind if we compare notes?"

I must have looked a little startled. It was Troy standing next to me, with his mile-by-mile in his hand. I nodded.

He sat next to me, not too close. "We haven't talked," he said.

"I know," I told him. "It's not that easy."

"I understand," he said. "We can take our time. But we really should compare notes. We're going to need to work together running the rapids."

"I know."

"I think we should probably scout Badger. It's a 7."

"That's at lower water," I said. "It's a 5 at this level. It must be tougher at lower water levels because more rocks are showing."

"I should have figured that out," he said. "I saw there were four rating numbers for each rapid, but I didn't take the time to figure out what that was all about. The numbers we want are the ones for high water, right?"

I nodded. "I'd still like to scout Badger," I told him. "Remember, this is practically new for me."

"But you were a natural with the oars."

"A few hours ago, you didn't seem so confident about me."

Troy ran his hand through his wavy blond hair and looked away. It seemed like such a practiced gesture to me. He was drop-dead handsome and he knew it. He looked back, catching my eyes briefly. "I didn't mean anything back there. It just came out wrong. I've forgotten how to talk with you, Jessie."

"Let's just talk about the river," I said. "I wish I knew what the water level was last October so I had some basis for comparison."

"I can tell you that. There was a graph on the bulletin board at the ramp. It was running around 15,000 c.f.s. when we were here last October."

Then he asked me, like I was worth asking, "Do you think everything will be easier at higher water?" He looked doubtful. He knew better, but he was working on being democratic, I supposed.

"I wouldn't mind that. Especially at Crystal. Let's check." I paged through my guide. "Here's four in a row that get worse at higher levels."

"Crystal's a 10 at all water levels, and so is Lava."

An awkward silence ensued. We'd run out of things to talk about, that quick. "I nearly forgot," he said finally, relieved at some sudden thought. "I brought something for you."

From the back pocket of his shorts he grabbed a pair of vinyl gloves and handed them to me. They weighed almost nothing. "Try 'em on," he urged. "They'll keep you from getting blisters. Great grip—even when they're wet."

"Thanks," I said. "That's really thoughtful. But what about you? You got a pair?"

"I brought those for you." He showed me his hands. They were all covered with calluses. "I did some rowing this spring in the Sierras. I could've used a pair of these when I started, believe me."

"So you're an ace boatman already. No fair."

He flashed me that killer smile. "Just face your danger and pull away, Jessie."

I was wondering if his advice applied *off* the river as well. "I'll try to remember that," I said.

"Just follow me stroke-for-stroke."

"I'll try."

"Well, let's go have some fun in Badger." He hesitated. "Jessie," he added softly, "it means a lot to me that you came."

Instant intimacy. The old Troy. "I almost didn't," I told him.

"I know. But you're here. That's all that counts."

It took us only a couple of miles to float under the bridge and down to where we could hear the "canyon tape hiss," as Adam had described the first sound of a rapid downstream. By then the walls of Marble Canyon had soared to six or seven hundred feet. As we drifted closer, the sound got louder and louder, and turned into terrifyingly ominous River Thunder.

Chapter

7

My heart felt like bombs going off in my chest. Badger Creek Rapid! I must be insane, I told myself, to think I could jump on a raft and row the Grand Canyon. My mouth was so dry. I asked Star for my water bottle and she passed it back.

"That's better," I mumbled. I adjusted my visor and checked my life jacket again. Think positive, I scolded myself. Concentrate.

A minute later Troy went over the horizon line. They were no more than a hundred and fifty feet in front of us, and they completely disappeared. I stood up one last time so that I could see the smooth, glassy tongue of current, where we needed to be. Miss it on either side and we'd flip in the giant pourovers. With short push strokes, I nudged the raft toward the brink of the rapid. Finally came the moment when we could see over the edge. I had identified the correct entry. We were picking up speed, so much speed, and heading straight down the tongue, right on the current line.

"Hang on tight," I shouted to Star as we dropped

down, down, and then sailed up and onto an enormous green wave like an ocean wave, translucent like an emerald and blending to white at the crest.

It was whitewater from then on, a tumult of crashing waves as we rocketed down the rapid. At one point I let my right oar get too deep, and it shot forward out of my hand. Tucking the left one under my knee, I reached as far forward as I could and grabbed the right oar by its grip. Shallower strokes! I told myself. I kept positioning to face the biggest of the waves breaking from the right, then the left, then the right again.

In my peripheral vision, the rapid was all a blur, a white blur. I was focused straight ahead now on the tailwaves. We took them head-on, each one, and roller-coastered over the top of each tailwave in succession. Suddenly I noticed Troy's raft. Those guys were all on their feet and cheering for us, including Troy. "Yee-haw!" I heard Rita shout as she waved her hat. Star stood up and screamed back, "We did it!"

No matter what happened downriver, this was pure magic. I remembered how much I was in love with moving water. What a feeling, taking a raft through a rapid. There's just nothing like it. I wanted more and more, and I was definitely going to have my chance. One rapid down, a hundred and fifty-nine to go.

That first night we camped above Soap Creek Rapid. Rita took charge of figuring out all the kitchen equipment, delegated culinary assignments and, when the moment came, announced her world-class dinner by banging on the propane bottle with the crescent wrench even though we were all right in front of her. Pug was especially proud of his trout hors d'oeuvres, which he carefully arranged on a platter with fresh lime. "Your presentation is artful," Star complimented him. "You've created something beautiful here, Pug."

The Big Fella was speechless. A shy nod in Star's direction was all he could muster. After supper, Star brought out some aloe vera for his sunburn and helped rub it on his back and shoulders. Pug was grateful for the soft, human touch. Afterward Star asked if Troy or I had sore muscles, and massaged us with one of her aromatherapy oils that she uses at the nursing home. I wondered if she'd chosen lavender with Troy in mind, or me, or both of us. She'd mentioned once that lavender has a calming effect on the Alzheimer's patients.

Rita, watching all this, announced that we were going to have a "ceremony."

"What kind?" we wanted to know. Rita told us mysteriously to wait and it would be revealed. She walked up and down the beach collecting driftwood, and then built a fire in the fire pan. When the fire was going good, she issued each of us a small stick. "This is last year," she said, holding up her stick. "It's history. We're starting from scratch. Okay, guys? Like we washed up on a desert island together. I just can't handle it otherwise. Everything will always be too complicated, know what I mean? Let bygones be bygones. I really think it's our best shot."

I wondered, Is this profound or is this crazy? Is it a really good idea or a really bad idea?

I looked around. The others thought it was a good idea, including Star, but then, she loves ceremonies in general. Troy, I could tell, was thrilled.

"We won't even *think* about last time," Rita elaborated. "It's like we got *amnesia*." She threw her stick into the fire. I thought, Good thing Rita doesn't have a license to practice psychiatry. Pug's and Star's sticks hit the flames simultaneously. Troy, with a glance my way, added his.

This was crazy, but forgiveness and lavender were in the air. "Make good again that which has been spoiled," I could hear Star thinking. Maybe this was the way to do that. I tossed my little stick into the fire and gave my heart over to the enterprise. Up in flames went my preconceptions and grudges, or at least I pledged not to dwell on them.

Troy looked at me with unmistakable fondness, as if a magic wand had restored our salad days.

It's the luck of Troy Larsen again, I thought, and then I chastised myself for thinking negatively. The key to survival on this trip has to be Stay Positive.

After successfully running Soap Creek Rapid the next morning, we entered a long, peaceful stretch where the cliffs pressed close and the river ran unfathomably deep. "What should we name our raft?" Star asked.

I looked around at the soaring walls. *"Senseless Acts of Beauty?"*

Just then, a canyon wren volunteered its own suggestion. We looked at each other meaningfully, and said the name at the same time: "The *Canyon Wren.*"

"Synchronicity," I declared.

"There are no accidents," Star proclaimed. "Troy!" she called. "Do you guys have a name for your boat?"

They conferred. *"Rental,"* Troy called back. *"Rental Boat."*

44

Rita hit him with the throw-rope bag.

"Hired Gun," Pug suggested. "We could call it the *Gun* for short."

"Guy-name," Rita protested, but she was outvoted. The names stuck. The *Gun* and the *Wren* floated through a few riffles and a few minor rapids, bobbing in the fast-moving current. As the walls kept rising, Star read to me out of the mile-by-mile guide about the rock layers. I'd made up my mind to learn something about the Canyon this time, not simply gawk at it.

Star had on her dreamcatcher earrings today, and had pulled her wavy reddish brown hair back with a beaded barrette. Not a hat person, she'd found a brightly colored river bandanna for the trip, one that had a sun visor built right in. She looked radiant, and ready for anything.

Just then I heard it again, the River Thunder.

"House Rock Rapid. We'll be stopping to scout, so get ready to land us, Star."

"The guide says it's rated a 7 above 35,000 cubic feet per second."

As we were beaching on the right, a professional outfit of rowed boats similar to ours had just finished their scout and was pulling out into the current. We tied up and ran along the scouting trail to a ledge just in time to watch them run. Their rafts were all yellow and a couple of feet longer than ours. Five of them carried three passengers each in addition to gear, while the sixth carried gear only. The name of the company, emblazoned in big black letters on each raft, was CANYON MAGIC.

The first to run, I could see, was going to be a woman who looked like she couldn't be any bigger than me. She had dark hair and a beat-up straw hat, and she was standing up in the raft now to get her last look.

What she was seeing had already rendered me numb. House Rock Rapid wasn't going to be straightforward at all—it was on a turn. The debris field of boulders that had been swept out of the side canyon on our right, during some monumental flash flood, had narrowed the river and forced it to turn a sharp dogleg here.

The main current, pushing left, led into giant waves along the cliff. The waves in turn led to two enormous holes at the foot of the rapid where the river was pouring over shallow underwater boulders and reversing viciously upstream. Either of those holes would swallow a boat.

The woman leading Canyon Magic's run did something that utterly surprised me. I'd expected her to float out onto the tongue, then point the front of her raft downstream and cock it toward the left shore, so she could pull away from the cliff. Instead she suddenly spun her boat and pointed her *stern* toward the *right,* at a forty-five-degree angle. Then she pulled, and pulled, and pulled again, with clean, deep strokes, looking over her right shoulder all the while. She was going so fast, adding her strokes to the speed of the current, that she broke completely off the tongue.

With her speed, she plowed through the shoulder of a big wave underneath a boulder and shot into the ribbon of safe, green water on the right, at least twenty feet away from all the violent whitewater. She was sitting so pretty, in fact, that she pulled her oar blades out of the water and coasted the rest of the rapid, well out of reach of the wave train and those two monstrous holes at the bottom!

I quickly looked upstream and caught glimpses of the next three rafts, all rowing downstream like she had. One of the boatmen, I noticed, had a flashy, peroxided streak in his jet-black hair. The fifth boat, rowed by a tall woman wearing a yellow scarf, made the same move but not quite as soon as the others had, and ended up on the edge of the wave train. She had to struggle to keep out of the huge holes at the bottom of the rapid.

The last to run, the boat carrying only gear, ran it the way Troy and I were used to, the only way we knew how. He cocked the front of his boat toward the danger, the left side of the rapid in this case, and pulled for all he was worth. He battled to get out of the big whitewater the whole way through, and barely escaped the holes on their shoulders.

"Man, that's fast," Pug was saying. "The whole thing doesn't take forty seconds."

"Troy," I said. "Did you see what those first five did? That was amazing!"

His arms were folded across his chest, and he was staring at the rapid with full-battle concentration. "Rowed backwards," he said, seemingly unimpressed.

Not exactly backwards, I thought. Stern first, yes, but they were rowing hard to the right, not straight downstream.

Pug snorted, then hawked a missile at a lizard on the rocks below. It missed. "Only one that had a decent ride was the last one," he said. "The rest took all the fun out of it. Only time they even got wet was early."

"Just think positive," Troy told me, with an ironic glance at Star.

Rita looked at the rapid, pantomimed terror, then looked back to Troy. "So what's my godlike boatman going to do? Do it like the big guys?"

"If it ain't broke, don't fix it," he said. "I'm sticking with what I know works. What are you going to do, Jessie?"

"Throw up," I replied.

Chapter

8

"Visualize," Star whispered to me, as we were riding the eddy back upstream. "Visualize a perfect run."

"It's going to go fast," I muttered.

"Slow it down in your mind."

Good idea, I thought. I took a deep breath.

Ahead of me, Troy was pulling out of the eddy and into the current to begin his run of House Rock.

"I've got it visualized, Star. Face my danger, pull away. Like Troy said, do what we know how to do."

"You're going to have a perfect run," she guaranteed me. "Don't worry."

I pulled into the current about fifteen seconds after Troy did. Now he was standing up and looking over the edge of the horizon line. I had about fifteen seconds before I would be at the same spot. For a few heartbeats I entertained the idea of trying the Canyon Magic trick, stern downstream. I tried to picture rowing downstream while looking over my shoulder.

I knew exactly what it would feel like: like rowing

backward over Niagara Falls. No, I'd rather see where I'm going, thank you.

I stood up to do my river scout. I could see the tongue of the rapid leading down over the edge of the first drop, then pushing left toward the dogleg. To the right, well downstream, I could see that ribbon of calm water where the Canyon Magic boatmen had ended up.

The River Thunder turned up like a jet taking off. I sat back down and started floating onto the tongue, just like I had in Badger and Soap. "Visualize whirled peas!" I yelled. Through the first drop, I kept the boat straight, then pivoted and started pulling. I braced my feet so I'd be able to row with my legs and my entire body, not just my arms and back.

It became quickly apparent I was rowing against some basic law of physics. Even though I was rowing my guts out, the current had hold of me and, like a slingshot, was shooting me straight into the whitewater in the dogleg corner.

We smacked head-on into the waves. They battered us from both sides. The worst ones, big enough to flip us, were recoiling off the cliff wall on our left. I adjusted to face them with the bow, and all the time we were shooting through a succession of mountains and troughs of surging whitewater. We were so far left now, we were only a boat-length or two from the cliff.

I got in two or three good strokes, still trying to pull to the right, but time had run out. We came over the top of a wave and I was looking straight down into a huge recirculating cauldron of whitewater. I barely had time, with all the strength I could muster, to pivot the bow downstream. We had to take the hole straight on, not sideways, to have any chance.

As soon as the raft entered the hole it was arrested. We were surfing in place on a churning tornado of water. Though I tried to push on the oars to propel us forward, I was utterly powerless. Amid the chaos and the roar, the heavily loaded raft felt like a toy.

Abruptly the raft was spun sideways, and the turbulence tore the oars from my hands. The downstream side of the raft lifted high in the air, just that fast. I saw Star go flying, and then I saw the raft tip past the point of no return.

More than the sudden darkness, more than the quiet, the cold, and the violence of the water, maybe even more than the lack of air, it was realizing I was under the raft that made me panic.

Wildly, I tried to break away and swim, but couldn't. I was pinned under the raft. I could feel my life jacket floating me up against the gear. My lungs were already squeezed empty from rowing so hard, and I was desperate for air.

I raised my arms and pushed myself down, but the turbulence kept thrashing my body around until I didn't know which way was up. At last there came a break in the turbulence. I pushed myself down again, walking along the tubes with my hands, kicking furiously. Kicking and clawing, I struggled toward the light. Then up, up.

I grabbed hold of the chicken line that ran around the outside of the raft, and tried to breathe in between the breaking waves. At least I was getting a chance to breathe.

Suddenly I realized *how* cold the water was. Someone was screaming my name. It was Star, from the other side of the raft. "I'm okay," I yelled back. I got a leg up on the spare oar lashed to the side of the raft and reached for the flip line that had been secured across the bottom. With the strength that comes only from adrenaline, I pulled myself, hand-over-hand, out of the water, then pulled Star up as well onto the bottom of the boat.

"I couldn't see you, Jessie! I knew you must be underneath! Are you really okay?"

"I'm okay," I managed, but I didn't believe it.

I looked downstream and saw Troy rowing out of the eddy to come catch us. Thank goodness he hadn't flipped, too. As they neared and their faces came into view, I saw a wild mix of emotions. They were scared, awed, amazed, thrilled—glad it wasn't them. They helped us onto their boat.

"You shoulda seen it," Rita yelled. "You guys got totally trashed. You stayed in the second hole for five or ten seconds before it spit you out."

"Felt like a whole lot longer," I managed to say.

Star gasped, "The *Wren* got her feathers wet."

We were shaking violently even though we were out of the water.

"The *Hired Gun* blasted through!" Pug exclaimed. "That was the biggest rush I've had in my life. They could charge a hundred bucks a ride if they could build one of those in an amusement park."

"Troy was like Arnold Schwarzenegger," Rita declared, big-eyed. "I was sure we were goners—then he made that last pull and it saved us."

What were they jabbering about? I could've died under there!

"Stifle it, guys," I heard Troy say. "Pull something warm out of our day sacks—even the rain tops will do. Can't you see they're freezing?"

Once ashore, I sat on the sand, utterly shell-shocked. I heard Troy say gently, "Take off your life jacket, you'll warm up faster. Are you okay, Jessie?"

I looked in his eyes. I saw only concern, no attitude. "I'm okay," I answered.

Two motor rigs came along, saw our flipped boat, and pulled over to help. The little beach was suddenly crowded with tourists swarming around like ants on a gumball. People were looking at me and asking about me. "I'm okay," I kept saying. They'd look at the overturned raft, then back at me, with doubts in their eyes written large as billboards. Their boatmen, with the help of about fifteen people, turned the raft back over in a couple of minutes. We'd strapped everything in so carefully that morning, we hadn't lost anything but some sunscreen and my visor and sunglasses, and we had replacements for those.

Troy thanked them in his casual manner.

"High water," one of the boatmen said in my direction. He was a big, burly guy with a handlebar mustache. "When we launched this morning they said we're on 50,000 cubic feet per second now—that's the record since the dam. Don't feel bad. House Rock was tough, real tough. You had to be brave to even try it."

I nodded my gratitude for his consolation. I didn't tell him this, but what I was thinking was, I have no business being here.

We camped right there, even though it was not marked as a camp on the mile-by-mile map. The other three told Star and me not to lift a finger. I'm not sure we had the strength to. The wind came up practically gale force and blew sand over everything. Star was fighting to set our tent up in the hot blasts. I wondered how she was finding the energy.

If we didn't get the tent up, the sand would blow in our faces all night. I made a feeble attempt at helping her, but when we got it set up, the tent pegs couldn't hold it in the sand. I held on to the dome while she collected four big stones and some tie-down straps from the raft. "Sometimes," Star said, "even the easy stuff isn't easy. Are you doing okay, Jessie?"

"I'm okay," I assured her. I wanted to go home, bad.

The others were cooking dinner. Rita's voice was carrying as usual. I heard her say, "No way I'd want to be one of the drivers. Too much responsibility."

I went down to the very end of the beach and around some boulders to a little sand spit. Once I was alone, I quit trying to manage. All my fear came to the surface. I started shaking. Knowing my confidence was gone, that was the scariest part. I couldn't stop crying.

Star came to console me, as I knew she would. I said, "Oh, Star, I'm in way over my head. This was a big mistake. I don't know what I'm going to do."

"Maybe you're out of balance, Jessie." She was serious. "Maybe your mind and your body aren't working together. . . ."

"It's the water, Star! It's just so overwhelming! Weren't you afraid?"

"Of course I was, but then, I wasn't caught underneath. I'm sure we can rise above this. If we've been putting out positive energy, it'll come back to us. It's the law of karma."

"What goes around, comes around?"

"I guess you could say it like that."

I chuckled ruefully.

"There's one thing I know for sure. You can't let fear take hold. You have to keep believing in yourself. I believe in you, Jessie. I really believe you can do this."

"Thank you, sister," I told her.

"And please don't say, 'Visualize whirled peas!' That's exactly what we got!"

After supper I walked downstream along some ledges where there was no sand blowing around. I sat and watched the hypnotic action of the water swirling underneath the ledges, and I watched the bats come out. Blasts of hot air coming off the superheated cliffs alternated with the first cool downdrafts of the oncoming night.

I heard someone coming—it was Troy.

"How are you feeling?"

"Beat with a stick," I told him.

"Well, you look mah-velous."

"I'm sure. I'm just trying to settle down—flatten out my brain waves."

"Good idea. I just wanted to lend a little encouragement, that's all."

"Sure."

"Just let me know if I can help."

It seemed he was almost comfortable with my situation. I was needy, and he was providing solace.

Quit being so small, I reprimanded myself. Give him a chance.

"I just wanted to let you know we've set up the solar showers on a tripod—used three oars. We even rigged a curtain with one of the tarps. The water's nice and hot."

"I'd love a hot shower."

He said almost gallantly, "You deserve one."

Chapter

I woke up feeling like fighting back.

I thought about my big mountain bike race last spring, my spectacular crash, and how fast I got back up on the bike.

I thought about skiing, about those downhill racers and their spectacular crashes. Those guys all get back up and come flying down the mountain again. They love it too much to quit.

Well, I love the water, and I love to row. The point is to get back on the raft and somehow get really good at this. Row like that woman who led Canyon Magic through House Rock. It can be done, I told myself.

At breakfast I barely spoke, I was visualizing so hard. Everybody could tell I was in a trance; they left me alone. As Star and I rigged the raft, I was already rowing in my mind. By the time we pushed off, I'd psyched myself back into a full measure of determination, if not confidence. As we raced through Boulder Narrows, I was riding the swells, crashing through the tops of breaking waves, spinning off the boils, walking the thin, snaking path of the current within inches of the monstrous eddies.

When it was going right, it was a dance. And, yes, it was going right again. I was dancing with the violent beauty of the Colorado at high water.

The river was so fast. We ran through North Canyon Rapid and Mile 21 Rapid, and suddenly we were in the heart of the Roaring Twenties. The river was jammed with raft parties and we were able to scout Mile 24½ Rapid with boatmen from all over the country—in their twenties, thirties, and forties, a few even older. They were juiced on adrenaline and more than impressed with the power of the high water, raving that they'd never seen anything like it and probably never would again. There was talk about Lake Powell, how it was still rising. People were speculating about how much water the Bureau might have to dump to protect the dam.

I made like a fly on the wall as they pointed out barely submerged rocks and waves and holes. I listened carefully as they discussed the nuances of what the water was doing at every conceivable location in the rapid. The exciting part was, I understood. I could really see what they were talking about. And I loved the jargon: rooster tails, curlers, reversals, haystacks, suckholes, all of it.

As we watched more than a dozen boats run, we saw two of them flip—saw the drama of people in the water before they disappeared around the bend. We heard the critiques. "Boatman error" was the consensus. Getting out of position; making a move a little too late.

It was big, big water, with waves taller than the rafts going over them. Mile 24½ Rapid was on a sharp turn to the left. I knew I'd have to pull early and with every ounce of strength I had.

When the time came, Troy and I both pulled it off. What a feeling, to bring a heavy boat through heavy water, then look back up from safety and see the rapid above you like a churning white staircase.

We'd been the last of the big flotilla to run. As we approached the next one, Mile 25 Rapid, we could see the group in front of us disappearing into it without scouting. Troy was inclined to "read and run," too. I told him I wasn't comfortable doing that since I couldn't see what was around the corner. Like 24½, the rapid was on a sharp bend. "I gotta scout it from the shore," I maintained.

When the two of us scrambled through the boulders and reached a spot where we could see the whole thing, my eyes were immediately drawn to a huge hole in the middle of the rapid. It would come up as soon as I rounded the bend. There was no way I was going to be able to Schwarzenegger the raft around that hole. If we dropped into it, it was going to be a certain flip, and that's what I told Troy.

Troy kept trying to talk me through it, telling me I could do it if I followed him stroke for stroke. I just knew I couldn't. I saw another group about a half mile below, dealing with a flipped boat. That's exactly what was going to happen to me.

My only recourse was to consider the Canyon Magic trick. I studied the water; I really thought I understood what it was doing. I visualized taking advantage of the speed of the current to help me make the cut I'd need to make to avoid that hole. In my mind I took every stroke of a stern-first run. I began to believe I had more than half a chance of pulling it off.

I thought better of talking to Troy about it—I didn't think he'd be receptive. But he asked what I was going to do. He was so invested in coaching me. I said, "I'm thinking of that stern-first approach."

He looked doubtful.

I said, "See that boulder just down from the top of the rapid, the farthest one out from our side? I'm going to try to cut downstream of that boulder, just catching that shoulder of the hole underneath it. If I can hit that spot at just the right speed, at just the right angle, I'll be good."

He shook his head. "And if you run into the rock? Or the hole just below it?"

"I know, I'd have to hit it just right. I think it's my best shot, Troy. I want to try it."

"I just don't think this is any time to get fancy, rowing backwards, looking over your shoulder . . . I'll end up picking you off the rocks. I really don't want you to do that."

He was way intense. It surprised me how much emotional investment he was putting into this. "Think about it," he insisted, and left me to do just that. He walked back to the boats.

I felt abandoned. For another five minutes I looked hard at the rapid. I visualized it both ways. I still thought I couldn't do it his way. For a minute I thought about giving up trying the alternative, just to please him. "That's ridiculous," I heard myself say out loud.

When we got out on the river, I didn't even tell Star

what I was going to do. I wasn't going to let anything break my concentration. Rowing hard, Troy disappeared around the bend and down into the rapid. I kept my eyes on that boulder barely sticking up out of the water, high in the rapid at the beginning of the turn. I was focusing so hard I could've exploded.

As I pivoted the raft downstream, I caught just a glimpse of Star's surprise. I smiled a fierce smile. I was already scooting downstream, looking over my shoulder and pulling with the current. It was all timing now. As long as I didn't row myself onto that rock or right into the hole . . . I let up for a second, then started to pull hard again, keeping that forty-five-degree angle.

The sensation of speed, all the speed I was building up, was entirely new and exhilarating. It felt like the boat was an arrow in flight, not the dead horse I'd formerly been pulling. I smacked through the shoulder of that wave boiling off the hole, exactly where I was aiming.

I looked around for a second, saw I was well out of reach of the big problem in the rapid. The boat-eating hole in the center of the river was thirty feet or more to my right. Pushing on one oar while pulling on the other, I pivoted the raft back around to let it ride through the rest of the rapid bow first. Star was going crazy, like I'd just run Lava Falls or something. It wasn't Lava, but it felt pretty good. What a sensation, feeling that boat scoot, when I'd made the cut at the top and found myself speeding downstream with the current like I was flying.

Star bailed out three buckets, that was all. What a feeling!

Troy didn't say a thing about it when we bumped boats

a few minutes later. He'd seen it, he had to have seen it. "Good going," that's all he said, and he said it flatly.

Good grief, I thought, would he rather have seen me flip? Coach gets mad when the quarterback improvises instead of running the play that came in from the bench?

For a few minutes, I let a small, dark mental cloud form. All I could think about was Troy, how he was blowing it, and how unnecessary that was, not to mention unfair. Then I gave myself a mental slap. Don't make so much of it, especially when he's been trying so hard.

We floated on through the cave-pocked cliffs of stunning redwall limestone, past Vasey's Paradise and countless other fountains spouting from the cliffs. Wherever the water gushed, the cliffs were festooned with hanging gardens of mosses, red monkey flowers, and maidenhair ferns.

Think about what you're seeing, Jessie. Remember, you came for the Canyon, not for Troy.

We floated past Redwall Cavern, the immense cave on the left, and we floated under the Triple Alcoves on the right. No more rapids today, only a cavalcade of wonders.

Star and I administered hydrotherapy to each other with the bail bucket. According to the guidebook, the water was forty-five degrees. For a minute after being soaked, I was freezing. After that, until my T-shirt dried out, I felt just right.

Everybody was going in for hydrotherapy in one form or another, including jumping overboard, except for Troy. Rita kept threatening to douse him but he kept declining. Finally she conducted a vote, reminding him

62

that everything was going to be democratic on this trip. He said "hydro" didn't apply. We outvoted him four to one, and Rita promptly let fly with five gallons of freezing water at his bare chest.

Troy didn't have fun with it, that was the disappointing part. He gritted his teeth and said, "I just don't like that, okay?"

Rita said, "Well, you aren't drinking enough water, either. The ranger said you should drink a liter an hour in the middle of the day. If you start to feel thirsty, you're already dehydrated. Don't you feel thirsty, Troy?"

He said calmly, "I don't need a mother on this trip. Okay, Rita? Just give me a little space, okay?"

"Okay, already," she agreed. "But think about it."

Pug, I noticed, was looking a little uncomfortable, like a kid wanting to leave a room when his father's getting angry. A raft is an extremely small room. The Big Fella brought out his fishing rod instead and right away caught one, which for all of us seemed a welcome end to an unsettling little episode.

Mile 36 Rapid was rated a mere 3, according to the guide, but what an awesome 3 it was going to be if the River Thunder reverberating upstream was any indication. Until we drew close, it was impossible to tell what was making all the noise. Troy, in the lead, stood up to scout it, sat down, and began to pull hard to the left. It was too late to get to shore for a better look. Mile 36 was going to be a read and run.

A few seconds later I could finally see what all the commotion was about. At high water, the lion's share of the current was racing under a low overhanging ledge on the right side. "Head-chopper!" Pug yelled back with all his might as he pointed to the hazard.

If I followed Troy's lead, and tried to pull away from that overhang the way he was barely managing to do, I might not make it. If we got forced under that ledge, everything above the level of the tubes including us was going to be sheared off.

"I'm going to do that scoot again," I warned Star. I picked the spot I was going to angle for, pivoted the raft, and started building up speed with the current.

It worked. I saw the horrific action of the whitewater on the ledge with my peripheral vision as we cleared it cleanly.

After that I used the Scoot, as I thought of it, at every possible opportunity, whether I really needed it or not, so I could keep practicing. I had a rush of hope that it might give me a fighting chance in some of the Big Drops, starting at Hance Rapid down at Mile 76. I realized that everything we'd seen, as enormous as the water had been, was going to pale compared to the Big Drops.

We made camp all the way down at Saddle Canyon, Mile 47. We'd put in a thirty-mile day, but we could have done more, the current was so fast. No sooner had we set up camp, the whole kitchen and all, than we heard a distinctive *chop-chop-chop* coming from up the Canyon. Troy craned his neck around to get a look. "Is that what I think it is?"

Rita jumped up, trying to spot the helicopter. "Are you sure you have a legal permit, Troy? Sure they aren't after us?"

"Maybe they're after *you*, Rita. Is there something you

forgot to tell us about what you've been up to back in Zoo York?"

A few seconds later a helicopter marked NPS appeared.

"Neighborhood Pool Service?" Pug quipped.

The helicopter hovered several hundred feet above, and we saw a guy wearing a Park Service uniform, goggles, and an orange helmet lean out of the passenger window and take a good look at us.

Then he dropped something out of his window, right into camp. It landed about thirty feet away from us. The guy waved as Pug ran for it, and the helicopter sped away downstream.

It was a bag of rice, with a note inside. The note read, "63,000 RELEASED THIS MORNING. CAMP HIGH. BE CAREFUL."

"Holy cow," Rita said. "Is this a joke or something?"

Troy muttered grimly, "They didn't look very much like comedians."

"Look," Pug said, pointing at the beach where we'd tied up the boats. The boats were floating fifteen feet offshore. We looked around at each other, and not a word further was spoken, not even a curse. Our fear was rising as fast as the water.

Chapter

10

There just wasn't any higher ground to retreat to that was remotely level. We had to take down the camp, rig the rafts—it took an hour—and head downstream. We kept looking, but we couldn't find anyplace campable. The camps marked on the map were all underwater.

With a pained smile, I remembered my father asking about the camp markers on the mile-by-mile map. He was thinking there'd be picnic tables and firepits and johns at those marked camps, like at Forest Service campgrounds. I explained that camp meant a small beach or any kind of level ground where you could set up your kitchen tables and tents. There were never any improvements. Once in a while the beach would be a couple hundred feet long. Mostly the shores were just rubble, so a marked camp was a prize and a thing of beauty.

It felt eerie still being on the river at dusk. We ran Nankoweap Rapid at Mile 52 almost in the dark. It had a hole in it that could have eaten Pittsburgh, but we heard it coming, kept hugging the right side, and avoided it cleanly. There were two high-water camps at Nankoweap, and fortunately one of them wasn't taken. We all knew we had to pull together or this was going to turn ugly. Everybody pitched in putting the camp together in the dark.

Nobody grumbled, nobody cussed the Bureau of Reclamation, not even Troy. I was so proud of him. He was working on his head, no doubt about it. Pasta primavera with sun-dried tomatoes and garlic bread was served by lantern light at eleven P.M. Fortunately the wind wasn't blowing sand around, so we could simply lay out our sleeping bags on the beach and forget about setting up tents. It was so much more comfortable to sleep in the open air, anyway, than in our tents.

To my surprise, Troy invited me to take a walk after we finished the dishes. I was swaying on my feet, I was so tired. "It's too late to crash early," he said. "A little walk up the beach would help me clear out my head. Look how much moonlight there is—we wouldn't even need flashlights."

"I would if I could, but I can't," I told him. "I'm totally wasted."

"Another night," he said, touching my shoulder.

Oh great, I thought. What's this about?

Don't make too much of it, I tried to convince myself, too exhausted to care.

The next day I did the Scoot in Kwagunt, the first big rapid we came to. I did it again in Mile 60 Rapid just for practice. We stopped for lunch at a side stream, the Little Colorado. I had my own name for it from before, the River of Blue. The water was still the same heavenly robin's egg blue, but there was so much more of it. The high water of the dark green Colorado was acting like a dam, backing up the Caribbean-like River of Blue. It looked like a turquoise lake.

During lunch Rita sidled over and whispered, "That thing you're doing really bothers Troy."

"What thing?" I whispered back, instantly feeling paranoid.

"That backwards thing. He keeps saying there's no point to it."

"You're kidding."

"Look, Jessie, we just don't want to tick him off, okay? He's been doing good."

"I know," I agreed. "But this is pretty strange, don't you think?"

"I know it is. But I just hate to see him getting worked up. He watches every move you make—you know that, don't you? And then he won't drink water, so he's getting these headaches. He's been popping a lot of pain pills. All he'll drink is a few cans of pop. Won't wear a hat, either. He's fryin' his brains."

Because it would ruin his hair, I was thinking, but I didn't say it. Instead I told myself to quit thinking so tacky. "I guess we can't make him do anything. Maybe he'll figure it out on his own."

"So?" she persisted. "You gonna help out here by not pushing his buttons?"

It struck me as strange that Rita of all people was bringing this up. Why was she worried about Troy's state of mind? "With this water, I have to do what's working for me," I told her. "And that's what I'm going to keep doing. This ain't no disco, in case you haven't noticed."

Just as we were packing the remains of lunch away, another helicopter appeared from downstream and flew past us upriver. It was followed several minutes later by a second, and then by a third. We stayed and watched, hoping they would clue us in. For the next hour, there were helicopters passing back and forth so fast we lost track of how many were involved.

Rita seemed to think that if we cursed them loud enough, they'd get the message: namely, that we wanted some explanations.

Troy was muttering now about the Bureau of Wreck-the-Nation, and I couldn't blame him. Enough was enough.

We didn't get any explanations. All we got, with no way to come by information, was a rising flood of anxiety. I overheard Rita, around the corner and under the shade of a ledge, telling Pug about how we were getting close to the Inner Gorge and the Big Drops. "I know," Pug said, "I keep looking at the map. I don't even want to think about what this high water's going to look like down in the gorge."

"Bad luck," Rita said. "Too bad this had to happen right when we're down here. Troy's lucky starting date wasn't so lucky after all."

"What's going to happen?"

I heard her smack him and say, "We're toast, big guy."

"I want muh muther!"

We proceeded downriver through surging rapids marked as riffles on the guide. Now that we were below the Little Colorado, we'd left Marble Canyon behind.

We got our first good look at the Grand Canyon

69

around Mile 65. After the confinement of Marble Canyon, the world had suddenly opened up. We were looking at a wide-open postcard view of the upper reaches of the Grand Canyon. From the dark lava flows at river level, the alternating cliffs and slopes soared nearly five thousand feet up through most of the colors in the crayon box. Pug filed his protest about the high water by mooning the Desert View Watchtower, perched like an ancient ruin ten miles away on the rim.

As we were approaching Tanner Rapid, the current swept us close to the shore on the left, in advance of a big bend. Up ahead, perhaps two hundred yards downstream, we noticed someone sitting in the shade of a tamarisk along the shore. The person suddenly jumped up, perhaps when he saw us coming.

He started pulling something out of a red duffel. No boats to be seen, just this one guy. He must have hiked in, I thought.

We were moving his way fast. The hiker was whipping out some kind of black clothing and putting it on, trousers and a top. Black? In this heat?

Rita yelled back at us, "What's the deal with this guy?"

Now he was putting on a mask, a black mask, and quickly reaching for something else in his bag.

A rubber sword.

He was dancing all around now, striking exaggerated martial arts poses. I saw a flash of red hair.

"That's Adam!" Pug yelled.

"Holy cow," Rita shouted. "I don't believe this."

"Interesting," I heard Troy say.

Adam whipped off his mask as we jumped out of our rafts onto the bank. Same old Adam, big head of curly red hair, maybe a few more freckles than I remembered. "So the Funhogs thought they'd run the Big Ditch without me? What's the deal?"

In the spirit of the moment, Rita jumped on him, like she was about six years old. "Man, am I glad to see you!" she exclaimed.

"I can tell, I can tell! Ninja attacked in Grand Canyon by girl in red bathing suit!"

Just to make sure he knew how happy she was, Rita kissed him on the cheek. Then she let him go and backed off, looking a little embarrassed by her outburst.

Adam had hugs for Star and me, and a handshake for Pug, whose face was lit with excitement. For Troy, standing by with the bowlines, Adam gave a neutral nod, that was all.

His face was more filled out. Now that I'd had a good look at him, it looked like he'd grown a couple of inches as well. He had more . . . bearing.

Adam was recovering his stride. "You got a little sun somewhere, Pug. What'd it do, burn off your baby fat?"

The Big Fella patted his stomach. "But I'm gaining it all back. We have food for an army on this trip!"

"So you guys can feed me? Good deal."

Adam started whipping off his Ninja suit. "Man, this thing is insanely hot. I wanted to make sure you'd recognize me."

He reached down by his duffel, grabbed an outlandish white baseball cap, and snugged it onto his head. It had a bill so long it might have shaded his navel, and a big

71

cloth flap in the back to cover his neck. He struck a pose with his jaw in the air and said, "So how do I look, guys?"

Pug was trying not to laugh. "It takes a real man to wear a hat like that, Adam."

Rita and Star and I couldn't keep from laughing.

"Got it in Page yesterday. Sort of a Lawrence of Arabia model—they assured me it would be popular with the ladies. It's just the thing for my skin cancer phobia, and in a pinch, it also serves as a tent."

"It's a fashion statement, all right," Rita agreed.

"So . . ." Adam paused, looking us over. "How's everything going down here? Star, did you see it in the tea leaves that I was coming? Jessie, how're you doing with the raft?"

"Swimmingly," I replied.

Adam's quick. "You don't mean . . ."

"House Rock."

"Sounds like I came to the right place to indulge in a little whitewater excitement."

Rita snorted. "Ha! Just so you know, we're all going to die."

"I see. . . . Well, now that we got *that* settled . . . How's this guy doing on the oars?" He gave Troy a poke. "Nice shades, mate. And the diamond stud's studly, too—it looks like you've gone Hollywood."

"Good to see you, Adam."

Rita waved her arms impatiently. "Let's dispense with the chitchat. Tell us how you dropped out of the sky."

"No parachute required," he replied with a grin. "I started at dawn from the Watchtower, down the Tanner Trail. Hoofed it hard. I thought today would be the earliest you could get here, even on this flood. Cut it close even so—got here only an hour ago."

"That's not what I was getting at," Rita protested. "You were working for Discovery Unlimited, remember?"

"Oh, *that!* Al let me come. I mean, after you called, Jessie, he could see I was eatin' my heart out thinking about you guys. They got me covered back there. I think he thought you might be able to use some help, tryin' to run this sucker on the flood and all."

"Flood?" I asked. "They're actually calling it a flood?"

"You wouldn't believe it. This is national news! It's on the radio all the time. Yesterday it was on the front page of *USA Today* with a photograph of the dam releasing all this water. I saw it for myself on the way down here. Talk about whitewater! It makes its own cloud, even a rainbow."

"They got the spillways going, too?" Troy wondered.

"You bet they do. They're blasting out of every orifice they got—the gates on the bottom of the dam, plus four huge nozzles shooting hundreds of feet into the river, plus the spillway tunnels, which they've never used before. The tunnels snake around the dam through the cliffs on both sides and blast into the river about a hundred yards below the dam. The whole thing is like special effects—too big to be real."

"Pretty," Troy said. "Real nice."

"It seems the Bureau of Rec really messed up this spring when they should have been drawing the lake down. In May it kept snowing in the mountains, then it rained a bunch and melted the snow, then it got real hot

73

suddenly . . . and all that water ran downhill a lot faster than the guys with the pencils had planned. The papers are saying they blew it because they were so gung ho on the lake getting totally full for the first time. Wanted to show off for the public. The Bureau is acting like it's not that big a deal—they're saying the releases are all within the design capacity of the dam, and all that."

"Doesn't sound like they're thinking about *us*," Rita pointed out.

"I hope you guys realize, you're running this river during an historic event."

"And you thought you'd join us?" Star teased.

Adam beamed that impish smile of his. "Tell you what I was wondering as I was hiking in this morning. . . . Am I the last guy riding into the Alamo?"

"Hey, thanks a lot!" Rita wailed.

Adam turned to Star. "Sorry about the negative imagery—I just couldn't help it."

"You're going to be on my boat," I warned him. "It's definitely the thrill boat. I could use some more weight to keep the front end down, especially with the big stuff coming up. It'll keep the raft more balanced."

" 'Balance' is the key word," Star declared, green eyes sparkling. "That's what we're shootin' for, all right."

"Enough jawing!" Rita ordered. "Let's go find camp. I feel like cooking supper. Oh, and let's get a few things straight, new guy. Everything's democratic on this trip except who's head cook and who rows the boats. Also, the guys set up the john."

Pug stroked his jaw. "I don't mind doing it, but I

don't remember . . . ah . . . *voting* on that exactly, Rita."

"Of course not! You're already doing such a great job filtering all our drinking water, I figure you might as well have it all. You're City Services! You know, water and sewer. You guys are our janitors in shining armor, and believe me, we appreciate it."

Troy, despite laying back, was hugely enjoying all of this. He looked genuinely happy despite the grim news. Like he recognized that Adam was the missing catalyst and now we were going to be okay.

"Oh, one more thing," Rita announced. "We had a ceremony. We burned up last year. No talking about it. Fresh start."

"What exactly did you burn?"

"Sticks."

"Ah, *sticks*. I'm not sure I would part with one of those." Adam looked around, and his eyes fell on his Ninja outfit. To our surprise he scooped it up and chucked it into the river. He was left with only his ridiculous rubber sword, which he brandished while tucking his free hand behind the small of his back. "I'm keeping this," he declared theatrically. "In case things get rough."

Chapter

11

I recognized the pinnacle peak coming up on the left, and the orange-red wall rising from the river on the right. We were approaching Hance, the first of the Big Drops.

Around the corner, the River Thunder ramped up and up. Adam gave us an expression of mock terror that was only half feigned.

On the left, a group of six rowed rafts, all yellow, had pulled out to scout. We knew we weren't that close to the brink yet, maybe a quarter mile away, but we could see their boatmen up on the talus slope. They were pointing downstream. Yes, they were scouting, from that distance.

We pulled hard to get over there. We wouldn't have known to pull out this soon.

Now I could see the lettering on the rafts. We'd caught up to Canyon Magic! I took another look. There was the pretty woman with the dark hair and the beat-up straw hat who'd led in House Rock, and there was the boatman, a Navajo or Hopi, I guessed, with the perox-ide streak in his jet-black hair.

Troy and I tied up, then skirted the commercial pas-sengers on the shore and climbed the slope where the guides were scouting. The youngest, with an earring and a bright red headband, was pointing out some feature in the rapid. His voice sounded nervous. Everyone looked so intense. I hadn't looked downstream at the rapid yet, on purpose. My heart rate was off the charts as it was.

When Troy and I found our own place to stand, a little ways off from Canyon Magic, I finally looked downstream to see what the roar was all about. "Omi-gosh," I whispered to Troy. "It's so huge, and so *long*."

As if to accentuate the natural drama of the place, the dark walls of the Inner Gorge began their menacing rise from the foot of the rapid.

Troy pointed. "There's a center run down the left side of that huge tongue. Take a look at the size of the waves down there on the right, especially against the wall!"

I brought my eyes back to the brink of the rapid. The key feature along the brink was a boulder that had to be the size of a dump truck. A quarter of the way into the river from the left shore, it was all submerged except for its long crown showing like a whale's back. The hole on the boulder's downstream side was the nastiest we'd seen yet.

If I could row off the tongue and catch the down-stream edge of that big hole without dropping into it . . .

"How are you guys doing?" asked a woman's voice. It was the woman with the straw hat. I'd been right back at

House Rock—she wasn't any bigger than me. Brown eyes, dark skin, most likely in her late twenties, real out-going.

Simultaneously Troy answered, "Doing good," and I answered, "Somewhat overwhelmed at the moment."

"My name's Kit," she said, and we introduced ourselves.

"Only the two boats?"

"That's us," I replied.

"Your sixteen-footers are so maneuverable. Ours carry so much weight . . . normally it's hard for the river to turn them over, but these aren't normal times."

Troy said, "We saw a lot of helicopters yesterday, when we were at the Little Colorado. Any idea what's going on?"

"We've got a two-way radio. The Park Service was evacuating all the passengers and crew from a commercial trip—a motor rig flipped in that new hole in Nankoweap."

"Must've happened right behind us."

She nodded. "Nanko's always been a nothing. But we're looking at 70,000 cubic feet per second right now, and the river's rewriting the book. We're not paying any attention to the ratings of the rapids. Like Mile 36—another nothing, but it's a death trap at these levels."

I could feel Troy's anger rising before he spoke. "Seventy thousand! Those guys at the dam ought to be hung up by their thumbs."

"I hear you, but at the same time, the guides who are down here for this wouldn't trade it for the world. This is the real Colorado, not the one the dam has been holding in check all these years. You won't catch us smiling—

too much responsibility—but secretly we're kind of glad to be here!"

"Interesting."

"Say, we should get going, but you guys are welcome to sandwich between our rafts if you'd like. Don't mean to dampen your wilderness experience, but you might want to consider it."

"Sure we'll run with you," I said. "Thanks for the cover. Can you tell us if we'll be able to find any camps down in the gorge?"

"Cremation shouldn't be flooded—there's all kinds of high ground there. It comes up on the left shortly before Mile 86. Cremation is the last camp before Phantom Ranch. There's a separate small camp on the downstream end."

"We'll take it," I said. "Thanks for that, too."

As we returned to the boats, Pug asked anxiously, "What's the drill, Troy?"

"Runnin' with Canyon Magic. They're going to cover us."

"My mother thanks them," Adam squealed from the front of our boat.

"Tighten the cinches on your life jacket," I told him. "And keep low."

"I'll keep my head down, like a victim of the guillotine. I wasn't planning on *watching*. I have a plan, wanna see it?"

He unclipped the bail bucket and put it over his head.

"Adam, remember, if you're washed away from the boat, stay on your back and fend off rocks and stuff with your feet. If you get caught up by a rope, remember you've got that knife clipped on your life jacket."

His voice came muffled from inside the bucket. "Yes, and remember to breathe air, not water. What else? First pants, then shoes. Lastly, always carry a litter bag in your car—if it gets full, you can always toss it out the window."

"Where'd you learn that?"

"In Crystal, last year," he replied, clipping the bail bucket back on its carabiner. "But we aren't going to talk about that."

"Definitely not. Now, if we swamp with water, I'll need you to bail that weight out of the boat so I can keep rowing. But don't bail until I say bail. Just keep hanging on. It's more important to keep you in the raft."

Troy motioned me over with a flip of his head. "Whatcha gonna do, Jessie?"

"My 'thing,'" I said. I said it apprehensively. I was afraid of how he might react.

"I'm glad one of us has a plan." Troy didn't look too good.

"C'mon, you got one."

He seemed so unsure of himself all of a sudden. "Have a good run," I told him. "Keep your sunny side up."

A couple of minutes later, Troy pushed off to follow Canyon Magic's third raft, which was rowed by the young boatman with the earring and headband. His was the raft carrying gear only, no passengers. The *Hired Gun* followed him upstream to the head of the eddy.

In turn, we followed Troy. A couple of strong strokes and the *Canyon Wren* was into the current and off to the races. My tongue all of a sudden felt dry as a stick of beef jerky. I realized I'd forgotten to get a drink of water at the shore, the way I usually did. Now Star was offering it, but if I stopped rowing, even for a few seconds, I'd lose my position behind Troy and mess up the tall lady with the scarf who was rowing behind me.

Kit was leading the whole parade. I felt so much more secure for knowing she was personally looking out for us, at least on this one. I took a couple of deep breaths, tuned out the River Thunder as best I could, and tried to visualize my run as I kept pushing on the oars. I was keeping the bow pointed directly downstream so I had a clear view of what the three Canyon Magic boats in front were going to do.

Kit was getting close to the brink. Now she stood for her last look. She was to the right of the whale's back and left of center on the river. Now she sat down, very deliberately, and cocked the boat with the stern downstream. She started to pull, and within a half dozen strokes she'd angled off hard to the left.

And disappeared over the edge.

All I could see beyond the horizon line were rooster tails spitting up from below, everywhere across the brink except at the center, where the tongue would be.

To my surprise, the second boatman wasn't going to follow Kit's lead and use the Scoot. He pushed frontward over the edge, down what must be the left side of the tongue.

The young guy with the earring did the same thing.

Troy, fifty yards ahead of me, stood up to scout.

I should've been right behind Kit, I realized. I could

have copied where and when she made her cut. Now I was going to be completely on my own, trying to pick my spot and time my move.

Should I just follow Troy?

I caught a glimpse of Star's and Adam's eyes turned around to look at mine. I kept focused on the horizon line, and the whale's back, and kept jockeying for position. I remembered what the big current had done to me in House Rock. I had to get off the tongue.

Troy dropped from sight.

I stood up to see what I could see. I couldn't see anything quite yet. Keep your nerve . . . you've still got a few seconds.

At last I could see down the tongue, and saw it bending to the right and into all the worst water. On my left, I could see the gargantuan hole boiling in the lee of the whale's back. It was recirculating so viciously, it might not release a boat after a flip. Cut too sharp, Jessie, and you'll drop the raft right into that keeper.

I sat down, spun the stern downstream, and started rowing with the current, hard to the left. We were building up speed, lots of speed.

We smacked through the big lateral wave pouring off the whale's back. Over my shoulder, I had an eye on the downstream edge of the hole.

Stop pulling for a second or you'll row yourself right into the hole.

Okay, *row!*

We were arrested for just a second by the boiling edge of the recirculating water. Good! I pivoted the raft, taking advantage of the braking action of the turbulence. It wasn't strong enough to pull us back into the big hole, but it would allow me to rest for a second, pull a few strokes to the left, and line up for the rest of the rapid.

"Flip!" Adam yelled.

I thought he was talking about us. But we weren't in any danger at the moment.

He was pointing downstream, way over to the right. "Troy!" he yelled. "He just went over."

I caught a glimpse downstream of the black underside of Troy's raft. I was back in the current now, shooting down the left center of Hance among big rolling waves, where I'd hoped we'd be. I had the bow pointed downstream, and all I had to do was keep making adjustments without getting my blades too deep.

"Bail!" I hollered. "Bail!"

Chapter

12

Cremation camp was aptly named. We were nine miles into the Inner Gorge and surrounded by its furnace-black, bristling walls. In no way resembling the sheer, clean cliffs of Marble Canyon, these walls were fractured into a million knife edges, and so steep it was impossible to see up and out to all the slopes and cliffs above.

The river here was narrow and unimaginably deep. No River Thunder to be heard, only the rush and gurgle from the interplay of current and whirlpools. The wavy green streamers offshore were the tops of feathery tamarisks drowned along the former waterline.

Rita appeared and announced that we had been invited by Canyon Magic to join them for hors d'oeuvres and also for dinner. "Well, did you accept?" Pug asked.

Rita went bug-eyed. "Are you crazy? After that flip, you think I wanna cook? Let's get going!"

For a minute, we thought that Troy was going to pass. Understandably enough, he was still brooding. He was sitting on a lawn chair, reading the mile-by-mile guide, undoubtedly dwelling on the prospect of the four Big

Drops we had to face in the next day or two: Horn Creek, Granite, Hermit, and especially Crystal.

"Aliens," he muttered. "What have they got that we haven't got?"

"Beer!" Pug told him. "Troy, they have *beer*. After what we've been through—"

"Talked me into it," Troy said good-naturedly, with a measure of reluctance still showing.

We trooped over to the other camp. It did feel strange to suddenly be among twenty-one people we didn't know.

It was also highly embarrassing for me. Their passengers—mostly fit-looking people in their forties and fifties—started swarming all over me like I was a rock star or something. Some of them had apparently seen my run in Hance, and the ones who hadn't obviously had heard all about it. Before I knew what was happening I was being handed a beer, a plate full of hors d'oeuvres, and a truckload of adulation. "Who are you?" "Where are you from?" "How did you do that?" "How long have you been rowing?" "How old are you?"

I saw Kit's straw hat from the corner of my eye. She had a grin on her face. I was trying to answer as calmly and as quietly as I could, picking the ones I'd answer—not my age—and playing it all down. I knew that Troy, though he was half facing away, was hearing all of this.

I confessed right away to my flip on our second day. "Where?" "How?" They wanted to know everything, especially the women did.

Though they were sneaking glances at Troy, they seemed to know you don't walk up to somebody who's flipped in the last couple of hours and ask all about it.

I was keeping my voice low and looking around for a way to get away. Troy was sucking on a beer less than twenty feet away and glancing occasionally at me. He and Pug were in the company of three of Canyon Magic's boatmen—the Indian guy with the flashy streak in his hair, the young guy with the earring, and an older, barrel-chested guy with a mustache and loose-fitting white cotton trousers.

The three professional boatmen were keeping an eye on my situation, and seemed to be quietly amused by it. A fourth, with a full, dark beard and wearing a turquoise T-shirt with stylized black lizards, was visiting with a cluster of their customers. The boatmen, I noticed, weren't drinking—only the customers.

A huge gust of wind suddenly came up and blew paper plates around, and sand in everyone's beer, including mine.

Pug was gesticulating wildly, ostensibly comparing notes with the young boatman who'd also flipped in Hance. Another gust of wind came up and blew a life jacket, down at their boats, into the water. The boatman with the lizard T-shirt ran down the beach to grab it.

Somebody yelled something about a tent, and I was suddenly saved from the little mob around me. A couple of people were pointing. I did a huge double-take when I saw what they were pointing at. Floating upstream on the eddy in a perfectly upright position was a yellow dome tent.

"Whose tent?" Kit yelled, and one of the tourists shouted, "Where's my camera?"

Nobody seemed to know whose tent it was, but virtually every one of those commercial passengers, as well as

86

the boatman in the cotton trousers, went sprinting for their cameras. In half a minute most of them were back, followed by the others. Everybody was cheering and generally going crazy at the odd sight of the tent out on the river. On all sides, shutters were whirring. Somebody yelled, "What's the brand name? Whoever gets the best picture can sell it to their catalog! Bet you anything it'll wind up on the cover!"

The tent was cooperating admirably with the photographers. It floated all the way up to the head of the eddy before it went down in a big boil, never to be seen again.

Then the guides got serious about figuring out whose tent it was.

Unfortunately it was Troy's. He announced, "I thought we'd try it out for a raft," but his joke sank like the tent. Then he said, "I'd rather sleep out, anyway."

It wasn't Troy's day. A couple of minutes after that, he slipped back to our camp.

I watched him go, and I set aside the beer in my hand. I knew better than to go after him. Suddenly I didn't feel like celebrating, and I sure didn't want to get tipsy and start saying stupid things around these people.

Kit had been watching me and pulled me away from all the commotion. She gave me a can of cold fruit juice and invited me onto her raft. She said it was where she entertained and also where she slept. "Too bad about your friend," she said. "Sometimes egos bruise easily on the river. There's so much at stake."

"He'll be all right," I said, unconvinced. I thanked her for helping us.

"I'm sorry you got mobbed just now. I should have seen it coming. They tend to treat us like celebrities sometimes, especially the women guides. It amazes some people that women can row whitewater. I tell them it isn't as exceptional as they think it is. So how old *are* you, Jessie?"

"Almost seventeen."

"Good for you. I was seventeen when I started rowing in California, on the Kern. The Kern was my neighborhood river—I grew up in Bakersfield. After that I did some professional guiding on Idaho rivers, but of course I kept hearing about the Grand—"

"How long have you been working down here?"

"Seven seasons. I got my degree in geology from Northern Arizona University in Flagstaff—goes perfect with all the interpretation we do for our passengers. Around twenty percent of the rowing guides down here now are women."

"How many times have you rowed the Canyon?"

"This is my thirty-first trip. I'm down here four to five months out of the year. For me, the Canyon is the real world, not the other way around. It's an unbelievable amount of work, but the people you work with are absolutely the greatest—so supportive. My image of heaven is the circular Grand Canyon. You get to the end and you're back at the beginning."

She read me like a book. She said, "You love it down here, don't you?"

"I really do," I told her.

"It shows. Where did you learn your downstream ferry?"

"What's that?"

"The move you and I both used in Hance."

I smiled. "So that's what you call it! I learned it from watching you in House Rock. I'd never seen it before."

"That's remarkable! That's a big-time move, a big-water move, and most of the private runners who come here from smaller rivers don't bring it with them."

By the time we ate, it was by the light of the nearly full moon. Troy didn't show. As we were finishing our dessert, the camp was suddenly invaded by mice. They were getting into everything, even running up the propane hoses onto the tables. People were shrieking and laughing and trying to chase them away. The guide with the lizard T-shirt and the big beard was saying it was because the beaches are used so heavily. People drop little bits of food on the ground, and the mouse population explodes. "Bad news for us," he said, "but great for the snakes and the ringtails."

Someone asked what a ringtail was. "Picture a small, slender raccoon—ringtails are in that family. They've got a catlike face, huge eyes for night vision, oversized ears, and enormous tails that have alternating black and white rings. Prospectors in the Canyon used to domesticate 'em to mouse their cabins."

Not ten minutes later, as if on cue, two ringtails appeared out of the tamarisks. They were much more interested in the garbage bucket at the edge of the kitchen than they were in the mice. The guide removed the bucket, but the ringtails stayed to perform. They played in the tammies, whisking their tails, chasing each other from branch to branch like squirrels.

I looked around at all the people and watched them enjoying the wildlife show. Pug and Star were sitting

89

together whispering, almost like they were a couple, and Rita and Adam were laughing about something. It occurred to me that the Big Fella had a whale-sized crush on Star, and that the Thief of Brooklyn and the former Ninja were also enjoying each other's company.

This was turning into a great party, and I meant to enjoy it. I popped a beer, then another. It was such a relief after all the work and all the anxiety. Whatever happened tomorrow, I felt absolutely grand tonight.

When I finally said my goodnights to Kit and the others, I found myself walking back not to my tent but in search of Troy. Tipsy-toeing to Troy's little clearing in the boulders. He needed consoling, that's what I was telling myself.

I found him awake, lying on top of his sleeping bag, shirtless as usual, with his hands behind his head, and looking up at the moon. I paused in the shadows; he still hadn't seen me.

He looked so alone . . . no one to care how he was feeling. I felt bad about that. I thought about how hard he'd been trying to "make good again that which has been spoiled."

I swallowed and stepped into the moonlight. His head turned my direction, I saw his smile. I came the last few steps.

Now that I was there, I didn't know what I was going to say. I could see he was pleased that I'd come. I said, "I just came to say good night."

"I appreciate it," he said, tapping his tarp alongside him. "Sit down for a minute."

"Just for a minute."

I realized my balance was off. I felt like I was still on

the raft, and it was rocking in the water. It was common to get those on-the-water rushes when you were on-shore at night, but now it was compounded by wooziness from drinking. I got down on my side, propped myself up with my elbow.

Troy put the index finger of his right hand to my chin. "Rough day on yours truly," he said.

"That's why I wanted to see you," I said. "To tell you not to feel so bad."

"I appreciate it, Jessie. It looks like it's turning out that you were the ant and I was the grasshopper."

"What do you mean?"

"Learning that move. That was clever of you, and took a lot of persistence."

"All the same, I was lucky today. From here on, who knows what's going to happen."

"We're into the end-of-the-world big stuff, all right. It's good to see you on top of your game, though. That's what I wanted."

His face looked so sincere, but I had my doubts. On the spur of the moment, I said, "Sometimes I thought you wanted me to flip."

He looked hurt. "Why would you say that? What are you talking about?"

"Forget it," I said. "I never know what you're thinking."

"You know what I was thinking about just now, before you came by?"

"W-What?" I stammered.

"Hiking out tomorrow, from Phantom Ranch, up the Bright Angel Trail."

"Seriously?"

"Seriously, I had it all planned. The rental guys could send somebody to hike down and row the raft out. . . . I was seriously bummed."

"But you aren't thinking about it anymore, are you? I thought we were both determined to make it all the way through this time."

"That's not my main thing, but hey, what am I gonna do once I'm out—go home and watch golf on TV?"

"I'm starting to think we can make it."

"You and me?" he said with a little laugh.

I gave him a slight push. "That's not what I was talking about."

"So am I doing better than last time, or what?"

"Of course you are. You know that."

"My therapist would be proud."

"You're really in therapy?"

"In L.A., everyone is. Even the therapists have therapists."

"You'll have to tell me about it, some other time."

"I will. Time is exactly what I wish we had. Everything's going so fast. We never get any chance to be together. It's all work, work, work."

"That's it," I said. "Bop till you drop."

He looked so . . . perfect. His blond hair, every feature of his face.

I watched the approach of his eyes, his lips. I didn't pull back. His kiss tasted sweet.

Then, like the heroine in a really bad soap opera, I pulled back and looked away, revelations of common sense washing over me as quickly as waves breaking in the river.

He whispered, "I've really missed you, Jessie. We've hardly had the chance to get reacquainted."

"Oh boy," I said. I got up on my knees and then stood up. I felt dizzy. "Troy," I pleaded, "I've been drinking. I'm sorry. I didn't mean any of this."

"Sure you did. Sit down, Jessie, let's talk. We have a lot to talk about."

"I'm sorry, Troy."

"Later, then," he said.

"Later," I agreed, and practically ran back to my tent.

Star was in there waiting for me. At the door, I said, "Make way for a fool." I got inside, zipped up the netting as far as it would go—the zipper had been sticking—and collapsed.

Star had a superanxious look on her face. "What happened?"

"I drank a few beers, went over to Troy, and wound up kissing him."

"It's not the end of the world," she said. "He'll get over it and you'll get over it. It's not like you killed somebody."

Of course Star would try to reassure me. What else was she going to say? Every way I could look at it, I'd dug myself a great big hole.

To punctuate the whole episode with the ludicrous ending it deserved, I felt something furry and scratchy jump right on my face. I let out a yelp and brushed it off. Star said, "What is it?"

"A mouse! There's a mouse in the tent!"

Chapter

13

The heat accumulating inside the tent woke me up. I heard the clang of a pot, not close enough for it to have been one of ours. After a moment of disorientation, I heard voices upriver and realized that Canyon Magic was cooking breakfast. A fresh wave of remorse swept over me when I remembered my disastrous visit to Troy. Had I been out of my mind? Our chemistry had been so complicated before—what was going to happen now?

I tried to sit up. My back had been stiff every morning, but this morning it felt as flexible as a slab of rock.

Then it came to me, the cost of sleeping in. We'd lost our chance to run Horn Creek, Granite, Hermit, and Crystal with Canyon Magic. We should have been up at the crack of dawn to make sure we were ready to run when they were.

Our kitchen wasn't even set up.

I must have moaned. Star struggled to consciousness and peered out the door at the bright sunlight on the crags of the gorge. "What's that cooking, bacon?"

"Yes, but not ours. Those geezers have more stamina than us."

"No doubt."

I must have been looking awfully worried. Star looked at me and said, "Jessie, don't worry so much. Remember, the universe is unfolding as it should be."

"I'll try to remember," I said. "What happened last night may have been synchronicity all right, but I have a feeling it was bad synchronicity."

Star and I got the kitchen set up, and we started cooking pancakes. Breakfast was an uncomfortable event with no shade to be had and the beach broiling. Everybody seemed depressed; no one was even mentioning the big rapids coming up. Troy and I were avoiding each other's eyes. Adam finally woke up enough to comment that we were doing a great impersonation of cows eating pancakes.

Rita finally kicked in. "Hey, you guys, look alive! Big day on the river, or did you forget? Jessie, Troy, eat some more pancakes, eat some more bacon! You have a little rowing to do!"

"Hup-hup-hup!" Pug chanted.

We all turned when we realized someone was standing there. It was Kit, in a clean outfit of tank top and shorts. She'd brought something on a paper plate covered with a paper towel. "Psyching yourselves up?" she asked.

Adam said quickly, "No, those are the only three words he knows. Just kidding, Pug."

The Big Fella looked a little sheepish.

"Hey, Magic Lady," Rita sang, "join us for pancakes."

"Actually I was hoping you could help us out with these leftovers." Pug was following especially closely as she folded back the paper towel. "Some apple strudel to go with your coffee?"

He whistled softly, then, "Wow, still warm. What a lady!"

She winked. "Is that a proposal, big guy?"

Pug was so taken by surprise, he forgot how to talk.

"Time to say good-bye, guys. We're about to pull out. Maybe we'll see you at Phantom—we're going to stop and mail postcards. I just wanted to wish you luck."

Kit said that with a special glance in my direction. I nodded back, but in front of everybody I said nothing beyond a mumbled "Thanks." She turned to go.

A few minutes later we watched their boats start to slip down the river.

Suddenly Kit was gone. I felt abandoned. The terror accompanying those words "Horn Creek," "Granite," "Hermit," and "Crystal" came creeping back from the edges where I'd pushed them. I'd thought Kit was going to take care of us. But of course, I knew better. Kit had a job to do, and we weren't her charges.

Back on the river finally, and only a half mile downstream, we pulled out for Phantom Ranch. No trace of Canyon Magic. We took the short walk under the giant cottonwoods, past a mule corral, to a tiny store and a string of rustic cabins. Somehow we were expecting more. We availed ourselves of our chance at cheeseburgers and wrote apocalyptic messages on postcards.

"Be sure you hit 'em with your rubber stamp, like the ones in the mailbag," Rita told the guy at the counter.

" 'PACKED OUT BY MULES FROM THE BOTTOM OF THE GRAND CANYON.' I want my brothers to see that."

A park ranger walked in. We asked if the releases from the dam were going to go down anytime soon, or if they were going up, or what they were doing. "I don't think anybody knows," he said. "Take a good look at Crystal."

"Oh, we will," we assured him, except for Troy, who said nothing. Troy was brooding.

Back at the boats and suffering from the heat, we took a plunge in the river. Even Troy did. He looked so nervous I thought he might shatter. As we were about set to launch again, Troy asked me how I felt. I was relieved that he was talking to me. I said, "My jaw feels like it's wired shut, I'm light-headed, and my stomach is doing loops. Other than that, I feel great. How do you feel?"

He managed his killer smile. "Not like watching golf, I guess. Good luck, babe."

I thought, Did I miss something? He just called me "babe"?

"Keep your sunny side up," I said.

A few minutes later we were bobbing down Bright Angel Rapid under the footbridge, with hikers waving from above. I stayed off the big rollers down the right. We raced through Pipe Springs Rapid and fell in behind a group of boats that had just put onto the river, probably after their lunch stop.

Star had the guide in her hand. "One mile to Horn Creek Rapid," she announced.

We realized we could already hear it. Adam stood up in the front and waved his rubber sword menacingly downstream. "We'll trim its horns, I say!"

Troy and I bumped boats for a second. "Let's stick with this other group," he said. "If they don't scout it . . ."

I understood his point already. "Then we won't, either," I agreed. "It would be awful nice to have somebody below us."

It was all we could do to stay on the writhing current line as we shot between the narrow walls of the gorge, jagged and black. Close to river level, the walls had been smoothed into intricate, fluted shapes, but I had no time to admire the natural sculptures. It was all we could do to stay close to those other rafts.

We heard the call passed back, from one of their boatmen to the next: "Read and run!" Apparently the boat in the lead hadn't been able to find a place to scout from the shore.

We saw that lead boatman slide down the tongue and disappear. A half dozen seconds later he showed up on the summit of a wave, and then disappeared again.

One by one, the rest of their boatmen disappeared down the tongue. Finally Troy did the same. What was down there?

Standing up on top of the cooler, finally close enough to see, I was amazed. Horn Creek Rapid was so narrow. Take it down the center, bow first, and shoot for the very top of each wave. Hit a shoulder and I'd slide off into disaster.

I sat down, then started to push the boat forward. The tongue was fast, so fast. It led down, down into a trough, and then we were looking up in the sky at the top of the first wave. I kept pushing to go over the very crest of it, and we did.

Instantly we were plunging, almost free-falling, into a trough that seemed bottomless. When we got there, which didn't take long, we were looking up to the top of the next wave, easily twice as tall as our raft was long. All I could see up there was sky, and I had little hope of climbing all the way up. But I kept pushing, and the current was surging powerfully underneath us—we sailed clean over the top, and down into the next trough. Way below me suddenly, Adam and Star were hanging on for dear life. Adam had that ridiculous sword in his mouth.

A few heartbeats later and they were high above me, almost straight up, it seemed. Star was screaming with delight and terror, just like she was on a roller coaster, which we were. We climbed five of those liquid mountains in all before the rapid spit us into the whirlpools. Eight boats counting ours, all sunny side up, eight bail buckets in action, whitewater-happy passengers all cheering, boatmen struggling to get the rafts under control.

Our boat bumped with Troy's. Pug threw his five-gallon bucket of water squarely at Adam. Adam retaliated in kind. Troy's smile was wider than his face, and I remembered that there was someone in there I liked. "Horn Creek!" he yelled triumphantly.

Shortly thereafter we saw Canyon Magic camped on the right, at the mouth of Trinity Canyon. There was no one to wave to. We guessed they were taking a hike up the canyon.

A few minutes later we could hear the River Thunder announcing Granite Rapid, also marked as Granite Falls on our map, one of the steepest rapids in the Canyon.

The camp on the left at the head of the rapid wasn't taken yet. It was only two in the afternoon, but we decided to stay put. With the fast water, we were at least a day ahead of schedule. We could rest up here and wait for Canyon Magic in the morning.

The camp was a tamarisk jungle, with shade everywhere, a big kitchen area, and plenty of sleeping spots. The constant roar of the rapid was intimidating, but we wouldn't have to deal with it until the next day.

"Wait a minute," called Troy. "Who'd rather run Granite now?"

For a second I was afraid he was serious, and so was everyone else. A slight grin appeared on his solemn face. Rita, who was about to buckle her life jacket to a tammie, threw it at him.

Finally a chance to rest. A chance for Star and Rita and me to get away from the guys for a while, and really take care of ourselves. We showered and shampooed and scrubbed until we discovered our former selves. When we were dry, we set up our lawn chairs in a little clearing in the shade and passed around a huge bottle of lotion. The sun had been especially hard on our hands and feet.

Rita had been wanting to braid Star's hair for her, and Star was delighted. Rita knew I could French braid and wanted to learn, so I got her started, then coached her from time to time. Mostly I watched the lizards, fat and scaly, play their lizard games as they chased each other around the tammie branches.

Rita claimed that the lizards doing push-ups had to be males. "Look, that one looks just like Troy," she said. "Flashy blue belly, orange highlights, lots of attitude."

I wasn't taking the bait, but Rita wasn't daunted in the least. "He still has a thing about you, Jessie."

I knew he did, but I sure didn't feel comfortable talking about it with Rita. There'd be no predicting what she would do with anything I would tell her. "I don't think so," I said. "That's all in the past. We burned up all those sticks, remember?"

"Mark my words. I've seen the way he's been looking at you."

"What way?"

"One minute he wants to kiss you, the next he wants to hit you."

"*Hit* me?"

"Hey, let's not pretend that some guys don't have it in 'em. Ask my mom. Ask Pug's mom."

"Troy doesn't have to be like that," Star maintained. "Pug, either. Pug told me he's not going to be like his stepdad, and I believe him. It's up to the individual, Rita."

"Yeah, yeah, gotcha. And a leopard can change his spots, too. Excuse me for saying so, guys—I really love you both—but sometimes I think you both just fell off the turnip truck."

"I may have," I said. "But not Star. She's seen it all."

"So much so she took to wearing rose-colored glasses?"

Star looked over her shoulder at Rita and said to her, "There's more to all of us than meets the eye, isn't there, Rita?"

I wondered, had Star just agreed with her or disagreed?

"Exactly," Rita said. "That's exactly what I've been saying. There's all this stuff going on that doesn't meet the eye. Some of it I worry about, like what's going on between Troy and Jessie."

"Don't worry," I assured her. "There's nothing going on."

"Then you'll have to explain something to me," she said, and she reached for her personal ammo can.

Star and I exchanged glances as Rita pulled out a folded piece of paper from under her instant camera.

She handed it to me, and I unfolded it. It was a photocopy of my Web home page, with my picture and all on it. "Hey, where'd you get this?" I asked.

"I found it by accident in Troy's ammo can this afternoon. I was going to borrow some lip stuff—I hate asking him for it all the time."

"Troy had this?"

"Sure did. So what's the deal? You guys have been in touch all this time? The two of you cooked up this trip together, or what?"

I looked immediately to Star. For a second, she was even wondering the same thing.

"Of course n-not," I stammered. "He must have got it off the Internet—the World Wide Web."

"You're kidding—World Wide? You put all this personal stuff out to the world? All about your dad and your stepmom getting married, about Star, about your mom dying when you were a kid, about your hopes and dreams? About our Grand Canyon trip last fall?"

My eyes returned to the page. I felt light-headed. She was right. Here was my life story, even the parts I hadn't lived yet, like the mountain bike race I was training for. I could even see where I'd written, "I'd give anything for a second chance at the Grand Canyon."

"It's just a form of self-expression," I said lamely. "All kinds of kids do it."

"I've heard about it, but I've never actually seen anyone's home page before," Rita said. "Takes deep pockets to have one, from what I hear."

"Hey, it's free, Rita—at least for me it was. My dad's hooked up at home because of the university."

"So you just send this stuff out into the world, and you don't even know who's picking up on it? You even gave your location. You say here, you live near Boulder, Colorado. I mean, I don't even have a computer, but if I did—"

"I was just sitting in my room typing this stuff," I said. "It was like writing a poem or something. And when you write a poem, it's nice to have an audience. The audience seemed so vague, and so friendly . . ."

"So Troy must have taken this off the World Wide Net, or whatever you call it. That means he was looking for you. Maybe he looked up the rest of us, too, to see if we had a home page, but I kind of doubt it. See? What did I tell you? He still has a thing about you, a weird thing."

Chapter

14

Star is always on the lookout for signs. As we were eating supper, and the river turned suddenly from emerald green to red, she glanced at me significantly. I knew what she was thinking. The river was telling us something.

"It hasn't been raining," Troy said. "Not even a cloud in the sky. So how'd the red sand get in the river?"

"Maybe it's been raining way up the Little Colorado," I suggested. "I've seen it on a map—it's more than a hundred miles long."

Adam was stroking his chin. "Dunno, could be blood."

Pug was pondering that possibility, almost fondly. Star said, "Red is the Colorado's natural color. The Spanish named it the Red River. So the natural color is a good sign."

Our redhead pointed his index finger aloft with a philosophical flourish. "Socrates would ask, 'Is the natural always good?' "

"Of course it is," Star maintained.

"An asteroid five miles in diameter strikes the earth. *Ka-boom!* Ninety percent of the species on earth go extinct."

"It's good in the long run."

"And how about when it's not dinosaurs but the human race we're talking about?"

They went on, but I wasn't listening anymore. All I could think about was Troy and my home page. Rita was serving the triple-chocolate cake she'd baked in the Dutch oven, but I hardly remembered to taste the chocolate, I had so much on my mind.

At last everyone went to their sleeping areas in the tammies, including Troy. I had some questions I wanted to ask him, so once again I walked to his little area by moonlight. Only this time I wasn't tipsy, and this time I wasn't feeling sorry for him.

His diamond stud was sparkling in the moonlight; he was resting on his pillow, just like before. Delighted to see me, not really surprised. He patted his ground cloth next to him. It was obvious he assumed I'd fallen back under his spell. When he took a better look at my troubled face and saw I was holding up a piece of paper, his face clouded. "What's the matter?" he asked. "Is something wrong, Jessie?"

"I don't want you to go blaming Rita for giving this to me. She found it by accident. I just want to know what you were doing with my home page, Troy."

"Please, sit down." He sat up while pointing me to his lawn chair, which had a towel thrown over the back.

"I think you should explain this," I said. My voice sounded high-pitched and emotional. I told myself to settle down.

He shrugged. "I got it off the Web, what do you think?"

"Why? How?"

"I just typed in your name one day. I was curious, that's all."

"It couldn't have been that easy. How did you find me?"

"University of Colorado at Boulder—I knew your dad worked there. And bingo—there you were."

"But why? Why were you looking for me?"

"I just wondered how you were doing, what you were doing. And suddenly there you were, right on my screen. It was a lot easier than dialing you up on the phone."

"I would have hung up on you."

"That's what I was afraid of."

"So, was that really you I saw in Boulder?"

He looked startled. "What are you talking about?"

Was he feigning surprise? I was watching closely, but I couldn't tell. "At the bike race," I said. "I thought I saw you in the crowd near the bottom of the mountain."

"Impossible. I was in California."

"You're telling the truth?"

"Of course I am. You said on your page that you were training for a race—so, how'd you do?"

I hesitated, trying to read him. "I won it."

"That doesn't surprise me. You're golden, Jessie. You know, maybe you could have a future in mountain-bike racing. I've been following the pros in the mags. Some of them are making in the high six figures—nearly a million a year. Women, too."

"I knew that," I said. "But that's not what we're talking about. We're talking about you having this in your ammo can. Nobody else's home page, just mine."

"Hey, nobody else *had* a home page."

I wondered if he knew that for a fact. "Star does," I said, which wasn't true.

He shrugged. "Not that I could find."

"It's like you were spying on me through the computer, Troy."

"I wouldn't call it that, Jessie. But while we're on the subject, you shouldn't put so much information about yourself on there. You never know who's downloading you."

"You're giving me advice?" My voice was getting shrill.

He backpedaled. "Look, Jessie, to be perfectly honest—"

"I hate it when people say, 'To be perfectly honest.' It makes me suspect the opposite."

"Look, you said in there that you'd give anything for a second chance at the Canyon. That's where I got this whole idea."

This time I knew he was telling the truth. I'd done this to myself.

"Then this whole thing is about me? This whole trip?"

"Sure it is. I mean, I like the rest of these guys well enough, but not enough to do all of this for them. This whole thing, it's for you."

"You see this as a present, a really big present?"

"That's right. Except the high-water part. I didn't know that was going to be part of the package."

"And you're part of the package?"

"I hoped to be, obviously."

"Why didn't you buy me a foreign country while you were at it?"

"You'd rather take the Canyon any day." Now he was smiling.

"What about other girls? Why didn't you take some other girl down the Canyon?"

"Other girls? Been there, done that. Other girls aren't you, that shouldn't be so hard to explain. I missed you, I wanted to be with you."

"No strings attached, supposedly."

"That's right. Just give me a chance, that's all I'm asking."

"I can't believe the trouble you went through to arrange this, and then you talk about 'no strings.' I still can't believe the letter you wrote, when you were pretending to be Al."

"What about it?"

"Like, 'all of us bought into the alternate reality Troy created.' Like, 'Troy was able to unite us as adversaries to the program, especially the girls.' "

"Oh, that. I admit, it's embarrassing. But I knew it had to sound like Al. The 'alternate reality' bit, that's a phrase my therapist always uses."

"To describe your schemes, I'm sure, which are mostly fantasy."

"I guess you could say that. But I'm working on it, Jessie, I really am. It's not like I'm happy with the way I am. I'm out of school and basically nowhere, and I'm trying to get a sense of where my life is going."

I was confused. He'd worked me around to feeling

sympathy for him once again. I didn't know what to say next or how to end this.

"Let's just run the river together," he said, as if reading my mind. "See what happens. Just give me a chance."

"Okay," I said. "Just tell the truth from here on out, okay?"

"Got it. Good luck in Granite tomorrow morning."

We were scouting when Canyon Magic tied up and joined us. Granite was steep, fast, explosive. I was thinking that a run down the tongue and close to the wall looked too dicey. I was trying to picture a far-left run. If I could use the Scoot and drop the raft just downstream of a certain boulder, high left in the rapid . . . That first drop would be steep and sudden, but after that . . .

It gave me a big boost of confidence when Kit started describing the same run to one of their other boatmen. This time we learned all of their names. Troy and I shook hands with Ray, who turned out to be Navajo; Pack, with the powerful chest and thick mustache; Gail, the willowy lady with the yellow scarf; Tom, with the full beard; and Juke the swamper, in training on the gear boat. Ray asked, "You hear about the speed run?"

We wagged our heads.

"Three professional boatmen are on the river right now doing a solo trip in a dory. They're out to set a speed record. They left Lee's Ferry about eleven last night."

Troy's jaw dropped. "Wait a minute—at night?"

"Marble Canyon in the moonlight," Tom put in.

109

"These guys know the Canyon so well, they could almost do it blindfolded."

Pack laughed. "They know the Canyon, all right, but the rapids are all different at these levels. Those guys are really hanging it out there."

"Which ones will they scout?" I asked.

Ray had a glint in his eye. "Word is they aren't scouting anything."

"For real?"

"This is for real. They want to shave off every minute possible. The radio said a helicopter spotted 'em at eight this morning at Mile 61 already, the Little Colorado. They're gonna set a record if they don't hit a rock or something. The radio said to keep an eye out for them today."

"What's the red in the river?" Troy asked.

Pack pulled on his mustache. "Weird deal. They say the river's been chewing through the concrete lining of the spillway tunnels that run through the cliffs around the sides of the dam. Now the river's starting to chew on the sandstone. That's what's making the red."

"Spooky," I said.

"Exactly," Kit agreed, motioning her people back to the boats.

Everybody ran Granite a little differently. Fighting off the waves close to the wall, Troy had the most excitement. One wave hit him from the side and washed him clean overboard. Rita told me about it afterward. At the time, she didn't even know he wasn't rowing. In the heat of the action, she turned around to check on him and found he wasn't there. A second later he hauled himself aboard with a combination of his tremendous upper-body strength and a wave lifting him up. He grabbed hold of the oars and met the worst of the waves just in time.

Next came Hermit Rapid, and it came up quick. At the scout, all the boatmen, including Juke the swamper, decided they wanted no part of the wave train. It was just too big. All the professional boatmen were going to try to cheat Hermit on the left with a downstream ferry. Troy looked grim. He said to me, "I remember telling you to quit practicing that thing. I was a total dope."

I said, "I think we're both going to make it, Troy."

Troy ran a couple of boats behind me. I had a huge run, from center to left, down the route I'd planned. I'd just eddied back upstream alongside the tailwaves when Troy started down. Rita and Pug were keeping real low.

Troy was taking the big center run, appearing on the tops of the waves, pushing hard to get over them, disappearing in the troughs. Climbing the tallest wave, the fifth, he was having trouble. It looked like he was stalling out. "Go!" I yelled. We saw a good portion of the bottom of his raft as it was pitched in the air by a wave from the side.

But it didn't go over.

"Squeaked," Troy called as he caught up to us.

"It sure looked like you had gravity going against you," Adam remarked.

Troy's eyes were huge. He clapped Pug on the shoulder. "Here's our antigravity device. My main man threw himself on the high side, at just the crucial moment."

"Un-believable!" Rita declared. "That was *huge*! Hermit's history! Bring on Crystal!"

Chapter

15

Crystal . . . Crystal . . . Crystal. The name kept announcing itself like a drumbeat from the dark corner of my mind where fear originates.

Crystal. The guidebook said there wasn't even a rapid here until December 1966. A low-pressure system stalled out over the North Rim and dropped thirteen inches of rain over a period of only thirty-six hours. A mudflow of unimaginable proportions carried thousands of boulders in tumbling suspension, as if they were pieces of gravel, all the way down the steeps of Crystal Creek and smack into the Colorado.

Crystal. We turned a corner and heard its resounding Thunder carrying up the river like a deep-throated growl. As we drew closer, it became a continual apocalyptic roar. From below the river's horizon line, where the river angled right and disappeared, nothing could be seen except spitters jetting high into the air.

We tied the *Wren* and the *Gun* at a little landing in the flooded tamarisks. Rita handed Troy a bottle of water. He brushed her arm aside. "Drink it," she insisted. "Remember what the ranger said—a liter an hour. You haven't been drinking nearly enough."

"Let's rest the ranger," Troy snapped. "I'm just not a person who drinks a lot of water."

She pushed it on him again. "It's not like it's a matter of choice."

"I'm drinking pop."

"You need to drink water, too, Troy."

For a second I thought he was going to take her head off. Then he took the water bottle she was handing him and drained the whole thing, spilling only a little bit on the blond-red stubble on his chin.

He wiped his mouth and said sarcastically, "Thanks for sharing."

"You're welcome," Rita told him.

Pug didn't know if he was looking at a happy ending or the beginning of a shoving match, and I didn't either. Canyon Magic's boatmen were already climbing a scouting hill; Troy and I hustled to catch up with them. Our passengers started down the partly flooded trail through the tamarisks that Canyon Magic's passengers were using to get down to the edge of the rapid itself.

"Take a look at that, Jessie," Troy said under his breath as he stopped dead in the trail in front of me.

I turned to look at the rapid. What I saw made me feel like I'd been punched in the stomach. Barely downstream of the tongue, where the river was pinched to its narrowest, it funneled into a hole that seemed too big and too explosive to be real. Pure foaming, roaring, recirculating energy.

The passengers swarming on the boulder field, only yards from the hole, looked like pygmies compared to the furious white background behind them. The hole looked almost as wide as the river. The recirculating wave it produced on its downstream side looked like it could be three stories tall.

We caught up with the boatmen on top of the hill. "I don't believe it," Tom was saying.

Ray said, "You go in that hole, it'd be like walking into a helicopter rotor."

"Okay, okay," Kit said. "We know it's horrendous. Is there a run?"

"Nothing on the left," Tom said. "The hole starts at the cliff over there and includes all of the center and most of the right. There's only that strip of water on this shore—if you could only get to it and stay on it."

"But when you pull hard-right at the top," Gail put in, "that lateral wave coming off the right shore is stronger than it's ever been. It's like a fence. If you can't break through it, it will funnel you real quick right to the hole—"

"We better go down and scout from the shore," Kit said, "right beside the hole. We need to figure out if we can break through that lateral wave and reach that strip of safe water."

Troy and I followed at their heels. We crossed tiny Crystal Creek and hopped from boulder to boulder through the delta of rubble that had pinched the Colorado into such a narrow and treacherous slot. I could only imagine the size of the submerged boulders out in the river that were creating this hole as the river plunged over them and recoiled in that monstrous standing wave.

When we got close, it was difficult to hear over the Thunder. The boatmen were having to virtually shout at

114

each other to be heard. I was astounded by the speed of the river coming down the tongue, how steeply the tongue was dropping.

I ran upstream of the hole, past the passengers milling around in the heat and taking pictures, to the beginning of the lateral wave the boatmen had been talking about. Within ten feet of the shore, the wave was already six feet high and starting to curl back upstream. It grew quickly higher and more violent in its fifty- or sixty-foot run as it angled, straight as an arrow, downstream to the hole.

Kit, I realized, had joined me. I was about to speak to her, but suddenly people were yelling. I didn't have any idea what they were yelling about, but then I saw them pointing past us upstream. Over the roar of the rapid I hadn't even heard the motor rig coming, but now I saw it looming right there at the top of the rapid.

It was one of those thirty-seven-footers. In the last relatively flat water at the top of the rapid, the motorman was turning the boat around, cocking it upstream toward our shore. I thought, It's kind of late to change your mind. "What's he doing?" I asked Kit.

"Turnaround move," she said. "Watch."

"How come he didn't scout?"

"The big rigs rarely do. For them, it's cake."

The motorman gunned the motor as he let the raft drift over the brink of the rapid down the steep incline of the tongue. He was keeping the bow cocked toward us. I could see what he was doing now: driving upstream, toward the right shore, against the current. He had his legs braced real wide.

The passengers, wearing yellow slickers under their life

jackets, were sitting as low as they could possibly get, their backs against coolers and bags. Some of them were hanging on with death grips and others were looking at us and pumping their fists like they were on a ride at an amusement park.

The engine was screaming, but the raft wasn't gaining any ground against the current. As it swept past us and up against the lateral wave, I saw a few of the passengers' eyes getting big. They were realizing something was wrong.

"He's too far out there," Kit said. "He's in big trouble."

We heard the boatman screaming for everybody to hang on.

The lateral wave, breaking left, shot the big motor rig straight into the hole. On impact, the boatman was thrown to the deck.

The raft turned sideways in the hole, shot to the hole's downstream margin underneath the monumental breaking wave, then surfed back across the hole to its upstream end. The big outrigger tube on the upstream side looked like it would be sucked under, but as that was happening the boiling action of the hole spun the raft downstream and up onto the wave.

Thrashed by the recoiling power of the wave, the rig seemed certain to flip end over end, but it lost momentum and fell back into the hole. Suddenly it shot up onto the wave once more, fell back into the hole again. When it seemed this might go on forever, a downstream surge lifted the entire rig up and slopped it over the curling right-hand shoulder of the wave.

They were free. I saw the boatman struggle to his feet

and point the raft to the right. He still had a quarter mile or more of whitewater to run.

"Did you see anybody get thrown off that raft?" Kit asked.

I shook my head.

"Cake no more! It's a wonder they all hung on."

Kit signaled for the Canyon Magic boatmen to come up to where we were and away from all the passengers. Troy was with them. I saw Rita behind, among the crowd. She noticed I was looking her way and drew a line across her throat with her finger.

"Now what do we think?" Kit asked the boatmen.

I thought they were going to tell her they didn't want any part of it.

"We know how strong the current is," Gail began, "—and how fast."

"With a strong downstream ferry," Pack said with conviction, "we won't be out in that current. That's where our small boats have the advantage. I believe we can crack the lateral right here by the shore."

"Or a bump run," Ray suggested. "Keep your butt to the right shore all the way down, I mean practically on the shore. Keep taking shallow strokes, make sure you don't pop an oar on a rock."

Troy and I were exchanging glances but saying nothing.

"What the hey?" Juke said, pointing upstream. "Check this out."

Here came another boat that wasn't going to scout Crystal. This one wasn't a raft at all, but a real boat, a small broad-beamed wooden boat with a high-pitched, pointed bow and stern. Shimmering in the heat, it seemed a beautiful apparition, painted brightly in emerald green with a red stripe around the gunwales. "The speed run!" Ray cried.

The dark-haired boatman was standing up for his look from the river. Never for an instant did he or his two passengers glance our way. They were all business reading the water.

"Watch the dory, everybody," Kit said. "We can learn a lot from his run."

With one more look downstream, the boatman sat down, cocked the stern toward the right shore, and began to row. Downstream ferry, I realized. He's gonna build on the speed of the river and blast through the lateral just a few feet away from where we're standing.

The boatman came sailing off the top of the tongue, rowing for all he was worth. At first I thought he looked good, but then it started to seem like he was a little too far out in the river. He had too far yet to come toward shore, with the river pushing furiously toward the center.

When the boatman hit that lateral wave with his stern, he was maybe twenty feet away from shore. The wave out there was already tall and pushing hard to the hole. The dory rose up on it but didn't have enough momentum to go over the top. The wave surfed the dory sideways and slung it into the maw of the hole.

I saw the boatman pivot the boat at the last second in order to meet the towering white wall head-on. He did meet it head-on. The dory was engulfed in an instant, pitched back and over. Bodies were flying—the flip had been instantaneous.

"Keep an eye on those guys!" Kit yelled. Tom and

Pack bounded downstream, leaping from boulder to boulder along the edge of the debris field, down to the corner where they'd be able to see farther downstream.

Five minutes later Pack and Tom were back. All out of breath, Pack reported, "We saw the three of them right their dory, midstream. Slick trick. Climbed out of the water, leaned back on those flip lines—over she came. The speed run is still in business. Three maniacs bound for glory."

Kit said, "Okay, guys, we know what we're looking at if we run. I've gotta bring up the word 'portage,' though we've never done it before. Crystal's never looked like this before. Safety has to come first. We know what a portage will mean—tons of gear to herk through the boulder field. We'd camp up by the boats tonight as best we could. We'd be back on the water sometime tomorrow afternoon. Or have we learned enough to think we could pull it off?"

"I still like that bump run," Ray maintained.

"If we portage," Pack said, "it's almost certain we'll have injuries among the passengers with all that carrying over the boulders. As we all know, most injuries occur onshore. I'm sure this won't surprise anybody, but I'm not as hot on the downstream ferry after watching the dory run. I like Ray's bump run idea. Start practically on the shore, keep your stern on the shore, keep pulling with shallow strokes, just don't pop an oar."

Tom pulled on his beard. "I can see it. I'm sure there's a run here. Just hug the right bank. Kit, it's your call, you're the trip leader."

Suddenly it got real quiet. Some eyes were on Kit, some were on the ground. Then Kit said, "The trip's better off if we think we can run Crystal and avoid a twenty-four-hour ordeal here. Personally, I think we have the experience to do it, and I like the bump run, too."

They all liked their chances, or said they did, even Juke the swamper.

Suddenly Kit turned to us. "Now what about our friends? Nary a peep out of you two . . ." She laughed. "I hope it's not out of respect for your elders."

Troy spoke up. "I like the bump run," he said, then joked, "That's my style—nothing fancy."

Now their eyes were on me. "I'm n-not sure," I stammered. "I might want to portage."

Chapter

16

Canyon Magic was getting ready to run, and we were going to stay put so we could learn whatever we could. In all the confusion, I really hadn't said good-bye.

Kit said they'd wait below Crystal for half an hour. Probably they'd be around the bend and unable to see what we'd decided. If we didn't show up within half an hour, she was going to figure we were portaging, and they'd continue downriver.

It wasn't long before we saw the first raft start to drift downstream. The peroxide streak signaled it was Ray. My mouth felt stuffed with cotton, it had been so long since I'd had a drink of water.

"Here goes," Rita said nervously as Ray began drifting down the shallows, keeping his stern within a raft length of shore. I saw how gingerly he was managing that downstream oar. Quick, shallow strokes. Now he was picking up speed, starting over the brink into the riffles and bumping over the rocks barely under the surface. He kept his stern pointed at the shore, kept taking quick strokes. For a moment he hung up on a rock, and his passengers lurched but hung on. The raft started to swivel around out of position; then it floated off the rock. A few more quick strokes and Ray was back in position.

I glanced upstream. The boatman with the big beard was bumping over the edge. Tom.

Ray, close to us now, was drifting with his stern over the drowned tammies, just as they'd planned. The lateral was coming up and now he was pulling for the shore with all he was worth.

At the crucial moment, right in front of us, Ray smacked clear through the lateral. He was free. No chance the hole could catch him now. The rest of the rapid was his: fend off the waves and ride it for all it was worth. Rita sent them off with a cheer.

Tom timed his strokes perfectly down through the steep shallows, careful not to dig with that right-hand oar, then pulled hard and broke the wave close to the shore.

"Made that look easy," I heard Troy say. We sent up another cheer, and I started visualizing the bump run for myself.

Pack came bumping down, and suddenly a rock spun his boat clear around. His stern was pointing toward the middle of the river. All he could do now was push to try to get back to shore.

Pushing was ineffective against that current, even for a boatman as powerful as Pack. By the time he pivoted the boat around and began to pull again, he was being swept into the maelstrom. I held my breath. It took only a few heartbeats for him to get there. Once he hit the hole and met the crushing white wall of water, it was almost like an explosion.

"Flip!" Rita yelled. I saw the black bottom of Pack's raft and I saw swimmers. The raft surfed around in the hole two or three times; somehow it suddenly flipped back upright. It surfed back and forth, pilotless and without passengers, and then it kicked out the right-hand side of the hole. I caught a glimpse downstream of heads and life jackets in whitewater.

Right in front of me now, Gail was pulling with all the strength her tall frame could generate. She made it.

Next came Juke the swamper, all alone in his raft, a fierce expression on his face. He rowed delicately, then hard, and he made it, too.

Kit was running sweep. She was halfway down the bumps when her right oar flew past her face. Her oar blade had caught a rock. It took her only a couple of seconds to jam the oar back into position in the oarlock, but it was time she didn't have.

The current had her now. While her passengers kept glancing toward the hole, Kit was fighting for all she was worth to get back toward the shore.

The downward tilt of the current was just too extreme to row against—a moment later Kit was shooting toward river-center, and knew she'd lost the fight. "Oh no!" I cried.

Kit left off pulling and jockeyed for position as she went into the hole.

She shot across the hole and into the towering white wall head-on. It must have looked like rowing into the teeth of a tidal wave. Though the raft weighed a ton or more, full of gear and people and half filled with water, the wave exploded on it and flipped it in an instant as if it weighed nothing. My eyes were locked on Kit. Bodies went flying, including hers. I saw her dark hair and blue life jacket plunge headfirst into the hole, and then I couldn't see anything but the raft surfing bottom side up in the hole.

I could see her passengers flushed out downstream, all three of them, but I couldn't see Kit. "Where's Kit?" I screamed.

It had to be thirty or forty seconds, maybe even longer, from the time she went under until the time she broke the surface downstream from the hole.

The six of us looked at each other and couldn't speak. Not even Adam, not even Rita.

"I gotta get some water to drink," I said. "Let's go back to the boats."

When we got there, Troy said, "Okay, we got about twenty-five minutes."

"Think fast, Funhogs," Adam managed.

"Jessie?" Troy said impatiently. "What's it gonna be?"

"A third of them flipped," I said. "And they're pros."

Troy's face looked bony and drawn. He looked like he was suffering from starvation. His eyes were blazing like he'd escaped from an asylum.

"Their swamper didn't flip," Troy insisted. "He had two flips up to here. You had one, I had one."

I said nothing. But I was thinking, What does that have to do with Crystal?

"Just watch out for that one rock Pack spun around on, don't get your oars too deep. You'll be fine."

124

"You actually want to run this, Troy?"

"Hey, I don't *wanna* run it, I'm *gonna* run it."

Rita and Pug looked at each other, and they looked sick.

"How come?" I pleaded. "Why don't we portage?"

His eyes showed no vestige of their practiced calm. They were skittering around wildly. "Because it's too much work, and it's probably a hundred and fifteen degrees out here."

"Full moon tonight. What's work?"

"Because I think I can run it, okay? Because it roasted me last year. Because if I do it, I'll like the way that'll feel, okay? Where's your confidence, Jessie?"

"Please, Troy."

"Let's just do it, okay? I'm positive we can do it!"

I didn't know what to think. I tried out the possibility that he was right. Maybe we could do it, and then we wouldn't lose touch with Canyon Magic. I knew I didn't want to fight. If I fought and won, Troy might fall apart in the heat during the portage. It was only Day Seven—seven more to come, counting takeout day. If we could get past Crystal, the pressure would be off. Get Troy riled up now, no telling what could happen.

I stalled. "I have to go down and scout it once more."

Star was at my elbow. "You want company, Jessie?"

"I better look at it by myself," I told her. "Really concentrate."

Back where I'd stood with Kit, I kept replaying all their bump runs in my mind. Even the ones who'd come through the bumps okay, I kept seeing them pulling with all their might to break the wave in front of me.

Whether Kit could have done it, if she hadn't popped an oar, I'd never know.

But I didn't think I could.

I started thinking about the dory run—the downstream ferry. Use the current to build up speed . . . hit this fence wave with lots of momentum, not just rely on my strength . . .

I was grasping at straws. Was it possible?

Suddenly I knew I was going to try it. I even felt a surge of confidence that may have been blind hope. The dory could have cut sooner, I thought. Maybe they would have if they'd scouted. I picked out a boulder on the shore to use as my marker and made a little cairn of rocks on top of it so I couldn't mistake it from out on the river. The problem was, I was going to have to take the raft through a small pourover to stay on my line.

Afraid I had taken too much time, I hustled up the trail through the tammie jungle. Around a corner I came across Rita, pitched over at the waist and holding her stomach. "Rita," I said, "what's wrong?"

She wiped her hand across her mouth and then turned around to look at me. "What's wrong? Jessie, I'm barfin' my brains out over here."

"You?"

She sat down and started crying. "Jessie, I got this feeling I'm gonna *die* out there. I just can't get it together. I'm scared out of my mind."

"I'm sorry," I said. "I just thought you were—you know—fearless."

"Yeah, well, I'm sorry to ruin my image, but this is too much, even for me. Do you think we can survive this thing? I mean, you've seen what it does. . . ."

126

I sat down next to her and dared to put my arm across her back. I knew Rita wasn't someone you held like a baby, even if she was crying. "We'll be okay, Rita, we'll be okay," I said, not believing a word of it.

"Just don't tell anybody, okay?" She took a couple of deep breaths. "Don't tell anybody I came unglued. Especially not that I've been down here ralphing all over the trail."

"I won't."

She took a couple more deep breaths, threw her head back, and closed her eyes. Wherever Rita went for strength, she withdrew what was left of her reserves. "Okay," she said.

We began to walk up the trail. We caught sight of Star up ahead, on top of a huge flat boulder, doing slow-motion Tai Chi exercises. Her delicate arms lifting slowly, extending out in front of her, fingers pointing up. With her knees bent, holding her position, she was slowly turning full circle.

"She's centering herself," I said.

"I hope it works," Rita responded without a trace of sarcasm. "You really think you can run this, Jessie?"

"I think I found a way. I wouldn't try it if I didn't think I had a good chance."

"Well, so does my driver. You guys have nerves of steel."

"Don't I wish," I said.

127

Chapter

17

I got out the foot pump and forced some more air into the tubes. I heard Troy saying he wanted to go first. Drinking down my water bottle, I nodded my agreement. I sure didn't want to. One of those old gladiator movies came to mind: "We who are about to die salute you." I caught a glimpse of Star wrapping the bowline into a neat bundle. Focus, I told myself. I kept visualizing my run.

Star was mumbling something over and over like a mantra. I asked her what she was saying. "Fear is the mind-killer," she replied. She didn't look centered at all.

"Think positive," it was my turn to say.

Troy was ready. Grim nods from his passengers signaled their tacit agreement to this madness. Troy nodded back and pulled into the current. Twenty feet offshore, he spun the raft around and started pulling back, getting into position for his bump run. Pug and Rita were already in battle positions.

Star and Adam took their places in the front, got their holds. They looked back for instructions. "No bump

128

run for us," I said. "I'm gonna use my Scoot, like the dory did, only I know what I'm shootin' for. If I do it right, we're going to go over a little pourover. There's gonna be a big snap."

"Got it," they said.

I was already rowing out into the river, farther out than any of Canyon Magic's boatmen had gone. The River Thunder turned up, up, up. If sound could kill, we were dead.

We saw Troy drop sideways over the horizon line. He was right where he wanted to be when he dropped from our vision. Good luck, Troy, I thought as I started to race down the right-hand side of the current line.

Stand up. Look over the brink. Find that marker and that pourover. There they are.

Something caught my eye where I shouldn't be looking. Troy's raft going over down in the hole! He'd flipped!

Nothing you can do about that. Sit down. *Focus.* Cock the stern downstream. *Row!*

I was over deep water, out in the river but not too far out. I kept pulling with long, deep strokes, building up speed to the right as I looked over my shoulder. I was approaching the brink. Suddenly we were over the edge, off the tongue and plummeting. I kept my angle and kept rowing hard. Over my right shoulder I could see the pourover and my cairn on the shore. I kept rowing with fast, shallow strokes, flying down the steepest pitch of the rapid. We were right on line to crunch the pourover with the back of the boat. "Hang on!" I yelled, and lifted the oar blades high out of the water.

129

I braced myself. Despite the rigidity of the raft, we took a violent snap and I was pitched onto my back. But I felt the momentum pulling us through the small hole below the pourover, and I still had my oars. Struggling back up, I saw we were virtually on the shore, with the lateral wave coming up fast. The raft's stern was so close to the shore, all I had to do was take a few shallow strokes. We shot through the beginning of the lateral where it was soft.

We were safe.

For a moment I rested, immensely relieved and in awe of the hole in Crystal, so close at hand, as well as the three-story wave breaking back into it. Then I started to row. "Where are they?" I yelled.

"Can't see 'em!" Adam yelled back. "You just row!"

I started working to the right. Crystal was long, like Hance. There were holes to be avoided, I could see, all across the center. I kept working right and got into a big rolling wave train down the right side. Star pointed. "There they are! Ahead of us, way over on the left by the cliff!"

I caught a glimpse of the black bottom of Troy's raft. Two people had pulled themselves up on it, but not the third. A major hole at the bottom of the wave train caught my eye. I started working to avoid it.

Troy's boat was at least a hundred yards ahead of us, where the river narrowed again, and it was moving fast. I spun mine around to face downstream and pulled hard to catch up.

"There's Rita!" Star yelled. "She's out in the river, way in front of their raft!"

Riding the overturned raft with Pug, Troy waved for

me to catch up. No matter how hard I pulled, I couldn't gain on them. Star was looking at the mile-by-mile guide. She said Tuna Creek Rapid was going to come up soon after we rounded the bend.

We rounded the bend and I could hear the noise coming from that next rapid. Then we saw boats on the shore, at the head of the eddy before the rapid. It was Canyon Magic, poised to catch Rita and our flipped raft behind her.

We caught the eddy and I managed to beach the boat. I was completely spent. On the shore, I fell in a heap while Adam tied off to a boulder.

Troy's boat was brought to shore next to the two of theirs that had flipped. One was already in the process of being righted. Canyon Magic was all business putting warm clothes on everybody who'd swum, and turning boats over. Shivering despite a rain-top and a wool cap, all Rita had to say was, "I'm alive, Jessie."

"Nobody's hypothermic," I heard Gail saying. "I'm just glad we had so many boats upright, especially the first couple, and that it's so hot out. Nobody was in the water more than about five minutes."

Adam, Star, and I went to help pull on the flip lines. Troy and Pug joined us. I took that for a good sign, even though Troy wasn't making eye contact with me and Pug was glassy-eyed. Kit, wearing a fleece jacket, was everywhere at once, making sure all the passengers were all right. I asked Ray if she was always the trip leader. "We rotate," he said. "This trip it was her turn."

As soon as the last raft was turned over, Kit raised her voice so everyone could hear. "There's a high-water camp at Mile 103," she announced. "It should only take us half an hour on this current to get there. We're going to read 'n' run Tuna, Lower Tuna, and the first three of the Jewels—Agate, Sapphire, and Turquoise. Let's get down to 103 before it gets late on us. Full moon tonight, everybody. Let's have an ABC party!"

"American Broadcasting Company?" a man called.

"Alive Below Crystal!"

As we were launching, Kit ran over and shook my hand. "I want to hear all about your run when we get to 103!"

Shortly after running Turquoise, I spotted a straw hat snagged on a tammie along the shore, in the eddy. I realized it was Kit's. We beached so I could walk upstream and get it. At that point all the Canyon Magic boats were ahead of me and Troy was right behind—at least he had been as we'd rounded the previous bend. But as we pulled back into the current, Troy still hadn't caught up. We were so close to camp, we decided to wait for him there.

"Should we unload?" Adam wondered when we joined Canyon Magic at 103.

I was looking anxiously upstream. "I don't know. Let's not do anything until we can figure out what's going on with Troy. Kinda long for a pit stop. I hope nothing's happened. . . ."

"He's probably airing out his head," Star guessed.

Canyon Magic's boatmen and customers had made short work of unloading their boats. Kit waved me over to hers and handed me a fruit drink from her drag bag. She was sitting cross-legged on the big deck in the front. "Now, tell me about your run, Jessie."

"I was afraid to do the bump run," I confessed. "I

just aimed for that little pourover with a downstream ferry and it worked."

"Right over it?"

"Right over it. Fast."

She laughed. "Next time I run Crystal at 70,000, I think I'll try that!"

"Was it awful in the hole?" I asked her. "It looked like you were down for a long time."

"Was it ever *dark* down there. I won't lie to you—it was bad, real scary. I was beginning to wonder, I'll tell you. Something to tell the grandkids, I guess, if I ever have any. It was definitely an experience in life, but not one to be recommended."

"Have you flipped before this?"

"Never on the Grand. I suppose if I had one coming, there's some consolation that it was Crystal at 70,000 that got me. It's a tough, tough level. I'm real concerned about what could happen to other people there—I just hope the water comes down fast now."

Troy's boat came into view. Strangely, he wasn't stroking toward shore. Pug and Rita were looking right at us, but Troy wasn't pulling over. I jumped up and said, "You guys okay?"

"We're fine," Troy called. "Going to find a camp. Hey, Canyon Magic—thanks a lot! Appreciate it!"

Kit said to me, "I thought you were going to camp with us tonight."

"So did I, but we never really discussed it among ourselves. I guess Troy figured we'd worn out our welcome."

Troy was already too far past to be able to pull over for the camp. So much for democracy, I thought.

"Well, I better catch up," I said. Then I suddenly remembered Kit's hat. "Wait a second, I've got something of yours."

I ran down to my boat and fetched it. Kit was tickled to see her beat-up old friend. She was about to put it on her head, then suddenly put it on mine. "I want you to have it," she said, and snugged it down.

When I started to protest, she said it had been given to her, and now was the time to pass it on. "Got backup headgear in my bag," she said. "Really, keep it. Hang on to it in Lava, though!"

A couple of minutes later, Star had the rope coiled up; we were just about to go. Suddenly Kit came running over with a little piece of paper in her hand, and stepped onto the raft. "We might not see you again," she said. "We're so far ahead of schedule, we're going to be doing a lot of long hikes now, and at least one layover."

I looked at the piece of paper. It was her name, Kit Herrera, as well as her address in Flagstaff and her phone number. "I've talked to the rest of the guides," she explained. "We want you to think about swamping for us sometime."

Chapter
18

It was nine in the morning. The shade was still on the gorge, but it wouldn't be for long. I had found a comfortable spot molded to fit my body in the polished formations at the river's edge. My perch jutted into the river barely upstream of our miraculous cove-camp with its plentiful sand and giant tamarisks.

I'd been sitting in my riverside perch since seven-thirty with no thought to rouse anybody or to do anything except enjoy the occasional canyon wren and the surging and gurgling sounds of the river. I was keeping track of the golden morning light as it descended the sandstones and limestones, visible once again now that the gorge was breaking up and starting to tail back into the river.

Alive Below Crystal. We were ten miles below Crystal, at Mile 108. None of us could have guessed we'd have this kind of luck, to land in an unclaimed paradise, maybe the best camp we'd seen the entire trip.

Looking upstream, I was surprised to see a flash of

yellow boats coming down the river. Canyon Magic, I realized. As usual, they'd made an early start.

The guides had the bows of the boats pointed downstream and they were pushing on the oars with a beautiful motion very much like pedaling a bicycle. I dared to imagine I might be in that lineup one day.

They floated by all in a row, soundlessly pushing downriver. No one called out to break the trance of the morning, and I didn't call to them. I just gave each of the boats a wave and a smile. But when Kit came by, she yelled out, "See you on the river, Jessie!"

I took off her hat and waved it. "See you on the river!"

As soon as the sun hit the cove, it became another broiling hot day. Rita wanted another day off from bossing breakfast. Adam and I made a mountain of French toast. Nobody was talking about Crystal or the events of the day before, or what was to come. Troy was moody; so were Pug and Rita. It was going to take a while for the effects of their horrendous swims to begin to wear off. Everyone was relieved that no one wanted to get back on the river. It was nice to have something we were so completely agreed upon: laying over and resting.

As Star and I were putting away the dishes, we heard Rita yell, "Hey, you guys! Come see this! Somebody left a big plastic lizard!"

Everybody went over to see her plastic lizard. It was about a foot long from nose to tail, with a yellow head, two black bands around its neck, and bright turquoise-blue beads all over its body.

"Totally lifelike," I commented.

"It's mine," Rita said.

As she was speaking, the lizard turned its head and eyeballed us, then blinked.

Rita jumped back and shrieked, in spite of herself. "It's alive!"

Troy had just turned away and was looking at something. "Check out the junk coming down the river."

Adam squinted. "Airplane crash?"

We ran down to the rock formations along the river to see what it was. A white lid from a huge cooler, a red dry bag, a yellow boat cushion, none of it within reach. "Crystal," Troy said.

More and more flotsam came down the river, and it wasn't long before we heard the sound of a motor upstream. It was two motor rigs, and as they came into view we could tell that something was terribly wrong. The first raft had forty or fifty people jammed onto it. The second raft had only the shredded remains of its huge frame and big boxes. It was carrying only one passenger plus the motorman.

As they pulled into the cove, we went running down through the tammies to meet them.

What we found, I'll never forget—a boatload full of people in deep shock. Some of them were moaning, a few were crying out in pain, but mostly they just looked lost, utterly disoriented and helpless. Some of them looked old—they could have been in their seventies. I saw all kinds of people with bandages, and blood showing through the bandages. The eyes of the boatman tossing Pug the line were as big as grapefruit.

The second boat, parking alongside, was a total wreck.

137

A woman tossed Adam a line. She lowered herself off the front of the raft onto the beach and ran over to help with the passengers. "What can we do?" I asked.

"We got people with advanced hypothermia. Help 'em into the sun, away from the river."

"I've taken all the classes for E.M.T.," Adam told her. "Let me help you."

"Work with Sam," she told him, "the guy with the red bandanna around his neck. Help him get the first-aid stuff off the boat. We've got a major triage situation here, and we've lost the first-aid stuff from two out of our three boats. Treat for shock; we need to get some splints going."

"Got it," Adam said calmly.

Three boats? I wondered. I was only looking at two.

The rest of us started helping people onto the shore and steered them up to the rock outcrops where it was real hot. Some of them couldn't move under their own power; they were so cold they weren't even shaking. Some were muttering incoherently, some couldn't speak at all. I saw people with their arms askew—fractures or dislocated shoulders, I guessed. There was a man still on the raft with a sharply broken bone sticking out below his knee, and a woman next to him stretched out flat with a bandaged head.

A boatman sprinting through camp with an ammo can in one hand and a two-way radio in the other ran by our sleeping bags under the tammies. He recruited Star to take our bags as well as any other warm stuff we could get our hands on to the people on the rocks. "Watch out they don't burn their legs on those rocks," he said. "Got any bail buckets?" he yelled at me.

"Two," I answered. "And two spares with stuff packed in 'em."

"We can use everything you've got. Even big pots and pans. We've radioed for helicopters—just got through about fifteen minutes ago. There's a landing spot right above you here, and I'm going to put an orange X on the spot for the choppers. We need to wet down that whole area to keep the sand from blowing. Anything that'll carry water . . ."

He ran up toward the flats above camp. We recruited passengers who were able to help, a dozen or so, and got a bucket brigade going.

Of their six guides, two were hypothermic themselves and out of commission. The boatman with the radio was on the hill making his X, another was staying on the boat with two people who couldn't be moved, and two, along with Adam, were giving first aid to the people in the sun.

As soon as we had the area on top wetted down, Rita realized that people were probably getting dehydrated. She ran for the five-gallon water cooler off the motor rig and told me to grab all our frozen lemonade from the dry-ice freezer on Troy's boat. There were a half dozen large cans in there, not frozen anymore but still cold. The lemonade mixed up fast. Rita had me throw all our drinking cups into one of our big pots, and she started off with the water cooler in one hand and the pot full of cups in the other.

I ran over to the triage area, where Adam was splinting a man's forearm. Star was rocking an elderly woman whose eyes were fixated on her. "What's your name?" the woman asked in a weak voice.

"Star."

"Star," she repeated. "Star . . . Star-bright."

As people warmed up, Troy and Pug and I helped them into the shade of the tammies. We could hear the *chop-chop-chop* of the first helicopter coming in. Green and white with the letters NPS emblazoned on the side, it flew down the gorge and made straight for the landing spot. It kicked up a terrific amount of wind and some sand as well, despite all the water that had been dumped up there.

"I found out what happened to them up at Crystal," Pug told us. "Their first rig flipped, and everybody from that raft ended up swimming a couple miles. That rig is still hung up on some rocks below Crystal. Their second rig surfed real bad in the hole. Their third rig came in right on top of it—wiped it out bad, and that's where people really got hurt. Some of the people from those two boats went into the river, too."

The two passengers who were hurt worst were stretchered up the hill. The helicopter took off a few minutes later. We raced to wet the area down again. Five minutes later we heard the second helicopter coming down the gorge. The boatman who was up there told us to stand back in the tammies. We helped with the next three people to be evacuated.

As it landed, the helicopter made a terrific amount of noise. A nurse stepped out, and behind him a ranger in a Park Service uniform and hat. The evacuees were walked, crouching under the rotor blades, and helped into the helicopter. The helicopter took off; the ranger stayed behind and began to survey the situation on the beach.

We had to keep the water coming to the landing

spot—it kept drying out fast in the full sun. Troy was fading. Rita told him he wasn't drinking enough water. I took a good look and noticed he wasn't even sweating. "I already have a mother," he told her. "And one is one too many."

"Testy," she said. "Needs hydrotherapy."

We were all on our way down to take a plunge in the cove when the ranger signaled us and said, "You're a private group, I take it."

"We're legal," Troy replied defensively.

The ranger smiled. "I'm sure you are. I wanted to thank you for helping out here. They can use all the help they can get. You the permit holder?"

"That's right—Troy Larsen," he said, shaking hands with the ranger and pulling himself together. "What can you tell us about the water? Is it going down yet, or what?"

The ranger grimaced. "Not yet. In fact, there's still over 100,000 c.f.s. coming into Lake Powell. They've erected a plywood frame on the top of the dam to try to add a little more storage. As of five A.M. this morning, they were releasing 75,000. I'd be real cautious, camp real high."

The afternoon dragged on and on as the helicopters kept going out and coming back. There were four of them, and the round trip took forty minutes. Troy had long since retreated to the shade of the tamarisks. A big private group came limping in during the middle of the afternoon with five rafts and three kayaks—sixteen people all together. They'd had three flips in Crystal, and they were evacuating a man with an injured shoulder. "Can we camp with you guys tonight?" a woman asked me. "Of course," I told her. Our spacious camp was beginning to look like the put-in back at Lee's Ferry.

In the hottest part of the afternoon, Pug came to me and said, "Troy says we're clearing out."

I looked dumbfounded, I'm sure. "Is he serious?"

"Troy's bummed about all the people here. He says we did all we can do. You know how he hates all this medical stuff. Says this isn't what we came here for. He wants to just give the camp to this new group since they need it worse, and go down and find another camp where we can have some peace and quiet. Said there's a couple of camps four miles down."

For a second I thought I was going to blow. I could see Pug was hoping I wouldn't. I realized Pug was just the messenger, and besides, I knew better. Provoking Troy wasn't going to help anything, and Troy had a point. I said, "I wish he'd talked to me about it himself, but tell him there's a lot of sense in what he's saying. Let's put down the kitchen, pack it up, and go."

Chapter

19

Troy woke up listless. He sat and stared at the river. No helping get the food out, no helping with the dishes, no talking about what we might do that day. After breakfast he went to the shore and started throwing rocks far into the river. It looked like he was trying to reach the other side.

Predictably enough, Pug couldn't resist the challenge and ran to join him. They got real loud, as if they were having an incredible amount of fun, but their mighty heaves kept falling short. Five minutes later we heard them declaring it couldn't be done. "It's much farther than it looks," I heard Troy say.

"Hey, Adam," Pug yelled, "come give it a try."

Adam ran down there, selected a few rocks, and on his third try, sailed one all the way across.

"It's just something I'm good at," Adam apologized as he ran back to finish packing the kitchen box.

Pug gave a few more mighty tries; Troy just quit.

Adam said to me, "Maybe that wasn't such a good idea."

"He'll get over it." As soon as I said it, I realized how much there was for Troy to try to get over.

"He's like being around a minefield."

"I know. Let's talk about you, instead. You're a man of many talents, Adam. Yesterday, during the big emergency, you amazed me. You were like a completely different person. So serious, so skillful . . ."

He laughed. "Lay it on me. I can use all the flattery I can get. It's a lot of work becoming an Emergency Medical Technician—I'm going to take the test this fall, as soon as I turn eighteen. I thought it would be a good way to get ready for Discovery Unlimited. It helped persuade Al to hire me, too."

Maybe that's why Al let Adam take off and join us, I realized. Al was watching out for us. He sent us an E.M.T.

"What are you going to do in the fall besides take that test? You're out of school, right?"

"Got a scholarship to Rice University, believe it or not."

"What are you going to be?"

"A Texan, I guess."

"I mean, what are you going to do? Are you thinking about a major?"

"Yeah, something really practical. I'm thinking about astronomy."

"Hmmm," I said. "I can see it. Big telescope, supernovas, black holes . . . just might be you."

We packed up and got back on the river. A few miles brought us to Royal Arch Creek and the short hike up to Elves Chasm. The name sounded so enchanting we had to see it. Troy was neutral but he came along.

144

The trail led around and under and over the tops of huge boulders. The handholds and the path had been worn smooth by thousands and thousands of hands and feet. Where the side canyon pinched shut, the trail led to a pool below a waterfall where the creek splashed a mossy path through an artistic jumble of colossal boulders. I could picture them tumbling end over end down the canyon and then suddenly locking into these exquisite angles of repose.

It took only a few minutes to discover that if we swam to the head of the pool, we could crawl under and behind a leaning boulder, then climb to a landing in the little grotto at the top of the falls. There, with the creek pouring through our feet, we found a perfect jumping platform into the pool below. We played in the cool shadows, doing cannonballs, scrambling back up behind the boulders, jumping into the pool again—around and around like we were the elves of Elves Chasm. Troy, though, sat in the shade in self-imposed isolation—no elfishness for him.

Everyone was talking about spending the day here, away from the heat of the open canyon, then heading down for camp when it cooled off. Though it shouldn't have been necessary—we'd already reached a consensus—Pug broached the idea with Troy, almost like he was asking permission on behalf of the rest of us. "Whaddaya say, Troy?"

"Fine with me," he said. "I like it here."

I was relieved.

A few of us walked down to the boats to assemble a picnic lunch, and brought it back. After we ate, Adam started scrambling around in the rocks and discovered there was a trail of sorts that led high above the falls. At one point he walked a narrow ledge, looking way down on us, and it gave me the willies. A few minutes later he reported back that there was another paradise up above with more waterfalls and pools, and maybe even a level higher than that.

"Higher levels of consciousness!" he raved when he got back down to ground level. "Ferns, flowers, cool pools! Let's go!"

Though I was trying my best to imagine places even more beautiful than this, I couldn't get past my fear of ledges. Looking absolutely straight down, like at the edge of a cliff, that was my nemesis. Everything blurs and starts to swim; I get all light-headed. I said, "I'm too comfortable right where I am, thanks."

Adam led Star and Rita and Pug up there; I watched them cross the ledge and disappear.

Which left Troy and me below. I hiked back to the boat and got a book to read, came back up to Elves Chasm, and found a spot in the shade. After a few pages, I must have nodded off. When I opened my eyes, Troy was sitting a few feet away, watching me.

I could see he wanted to talk. I spoke first, out of nervousness, I suppose. "So, how are you feeling?" I asked.

"Better," he said. "I had a killer headache this morning. I thought it was going to take my head off."

"Did you take something for it?"

"I've got some prescription painkillers with me. I'm feeling pretty good now. Sometimes I get these at home, too, and they can be just about unbearable."

"I'm sorry to hear that. The heat down here probably isn't helping—maybe you're getting dehydrated."

He nodded. I could tell he wanted to get off the topic.

"Day Nine already," he said. "Time's running out."

"I know. It's going fast. After today, only four more complete days. That last morning they pick us up down at Diamond Creek doesn't count."

"Day Fourteen is the first day of the rest of my life, as they say."

"So, what are you thinking about doing with it? Thinking about college?"

He waved that suggestion away. "Are you kidding? Me? I'm thinking about being a manager for a girl bike racer."

"Quit flirting," I said. "Seriously, what are you thinking about?"

"That *is* what I'm thinking about. I've got a great place out in California—right on the beach. I want you to come out and see it. It'd be a great place for you to train."

He's kidding around, I told myself. Don't let this get to you. "Have you forgotten I'm still in high school?" I said with a grin. "I'm not planning on moving to California anytime soon."

"No, really," he insisted. "I've got something I want you to think about. You don't have to say yes or no right now—I just want you to think about it during the rest of the trip."

"Don't," I said. "Just don't lay anything heavy on me, Troy, all right?"

"Listen, Jessie . . ." His voice didn't sound exactly affectionate. It sounded like a cross between demanding and pleading. "After this trip, you don't really have to get right back home or anything, do you?"

I knew I couldn't let him go any further. "Troy, it sounds like you've been working up another 'alternate reality,' and it sounds like it has me in it. I'm driving back to Boulder with Star as soon as we get off the river, and that's the end of it."

"C'mon, Jessie—we'd have a lot of fun. You could try it just for the summer, then finish high school in California if you like it. My place has a great guest room, windows out onto the ocean. What do you have to lose? Hey, take a risk—think big!"

I was stunned. This was much worse than I'd thought. He had this all built up in his mind, all planned out, just like he'd planned this Grand Canyon trip. And he actually thought it could happen.

"Whoa, Troy," I said. "Slow down, here." I didn't want to make him mad, but I didn't want to encourage him, either. I spoke quietly, trying my best to be caring but not lead him on. "We're not right for each other— that's the bottom line."

"That's not the way it seemed the other night."

"I'm sorry if I gave you the wrong signals. I really am. You've been trying to make this a good trip for everyone, and I appreciate that."

"You appreciate it? Jessie, that's not enough. This is hard for me to say, so just listen. I need you in my life, can't you see that? All I have now is a lot of stuff, a lot of expensive toys. My folks don't want me around, that's

148

for sure. I need someone for me, and you're the one I want. Don't you think I've changed, for the better?"

"Yes, I do, and I hope you keep it up," I said. "But I'm not ready to get involved like that, not with you or anybody. What I'm looking forward to is getting out on my own, after high school, inventing my own life. Don't take this wrong, but I feel like what you're hoping for is somebody who will magically fix up your life, make a life *for* you. Troy, that's stuff you have to do for yourself."

I could see I was making him angry. "So what's been the point to all this effort I've been putting out, if you aren't even willing to give me a chance? We're made for each other, Jessie, why can't you see that? How can I convince you? I even love the bumper sticker on your car, the one about Elvis. I used to have one like it myself."

"Elvis?" I repeated, confused. "But my bumper sticker says . . ."

Suddenly this all came crashing into place, and I felt a knot forming in my stomach. "What does my bumper sticker say, Troy?" I asked slowly. "The one you like so much."

"You know, 'HONK IF YOU'RE ELVIS.' It's you. That's all I'm saying. Cute, fun . . ."

My mind was racing. I had to get this out in the open, even though I knew it was going to upset him.

"You really *were* in Boulder this spring, weren't you?" I said.

"What are you talking about?"

"That Elvis sticker—it was on the Bug when we bought it, but we scraped it off a couple of weeks later.

149

It's not there anymore. You must not have noticed at Lee's Ferry."

"Okay, okay," he said, knowing he'd been busted. "So I was in Boulder. So what's the big deal?"

"You were at my house, watching me where I live?"

He hesitated. "Oh, yeah. Your school, the bookstore where you work, all of it." He had his head down now, and I almost thought he was going to cry.

A million thoughts were rushing through my mind. If he had even called, to say he was in town . . . What kind of person would go to such lengths, in secret? Was he going to keep doing this? Could it get worse? I knew I didn't want to upset him any more. I needed to be really, really careful, I needed time to think.

Just act like this is all normal, I told myself. Keep your voice calm, don't let him see you're scared.

"Then I guess that really was you I saw at the bike race, wasn't it," I said.

"That's right," he responded, brightening. "I saw your big crack-up and everything. Saw you get back on the bike and win. You were amazing! That's what I've been trying to tell you, Jessie. You've got no end of potential."

Just then we heard whooping and hollering—the hikers were returning. Not a minute too soon, I thought. My heart was racing like a train. Without another look at Troy, I ran over and dove into the pool, then found Star and gave her a big hug.

Back on the river, I barely noticed the classic Grand Canyon scenery as we floated down Conquistador Aisle. We were looking all the way up through buttes and mesas and temples to the tall trees on the rims, but I was

150

much too preoccupied to enjoy it. I could barely focus on the cluster of bighorn sheep Pug spotted standing still as statues on a huge boulder just up from the river.

Everyone was still in a state of higher consciousness, having so recently descended from the wonders of Upper Elves Chasm. How I wished I'd braved that ledge and gone with them.

Instead I'd stayed behind, and now I knew too much, way too much. I tried to convince myself not to worry. Just four more days together on the river, and then I could put him behind me forever. Except, what if he wouldn't let go? Heaven knows he could afford to push it even further. What if he moved out to Colorado? To Boulder? I wished I could talk to my dad.

What about everybody else on the trip? What had I gotten all of them into now? How was Troy going to react to our talk? Was he going to regret having admitted so much?

Remember to keep an eye out for camp, I told myself. We're less than an hour from Blacktail Canyon, and if we miss the camps around there, we're into another gorge.

Troy pushed methodically on his oars, revealing nothing of his state of mind. I suspected he was feeling an internal sort of thunder equivalent to the River Thunder at Crystal. And that was scary.

Chapter

20

I said nothing to Star about my conversation with Troy and what I'd learned. Best to tell no one, I decided. If they knew, they might act differently around Troy. He'd notice, and then what? I kept it all to myself and tried to act normal. Our camp at Blacktail Canyon had actually been fun. On the surface, nothing seemed any different.

The next day, as we fought our way through the big rapids of the middle granite gorge—Fossil, Specter, Bedrock, and Dubendorff—I was hoping that the passing of time might be working to our advantage. Everybody could really think about how far we'd come, what we were trying to do, and what it would take if we were all going to pull through together this time.

We passed Canyon Magic when they were away from their boats and hiking up a side canyon. It gave us a rush of pride to realize how many big rapids we'd been scouting and running all by ourselves, and putting behind us. On 70,000-some cubic feet per second.

We made camp on our tenth day at the brink of

Tapeats Creek Rapid, at the mouth of Tapeats Creek, Mile 133. The creek was running big and clear and cold like a Rocky Mountain trout stream. The camp was so perfect it took only half a second for us to reach a consensus that we'd lay over there and spend a second night. We could spend a day off the rafts and hike up to Thunder River. Under the photograph in the mile-by-mile, it said Thunder River was the largest spring in the world.

After dinner, Adam made a major positive contribution to the group chemistry. He hiked up through barrel cactus and the talus rocks on the slope above us to try to get as close as possible to a bighorn ram that was grazing up there. Even from a distance the ram was impressive, with massive horns that made a full curl.

The ram was allowing Adam to get pretty close, within a hundred feet at least. Down at camp, Pug was eating his heart out that he hadn't gone along. He'd never guessed Adam would get so close.

"It's because this is a park," Pug surmised. "They're never hunted."

We were about to find out how unafraid this particular ram was. Adam started blatting at it, like a sheep. The ram cocked its head, looked squarely at Adam, then came charging down the slope after him. Adam sprinted toward us, then held up as soon as he realized the ram had halted its charge. Adam went, *"BAAAA . . . BAAAAA . . ."* at the ram. Once again, the bighorn charged down the slope after him. In his retreat, Adam leaped a barrel cactus that might have been waist-tall.

The ram halted again, this time no more than a couple of hundred feet from camp. At half that distance, Adam had taken shelter behind a boulder, and now he scrambled to its top. "Adam," Rita called. "You don't suppose that sheep would—"

Adam glowered at the ram. *"BAAAA! BAAAAA! BAAAAAA!"*

I heard the bighorn snort twice, then come charging with a vengeance. Adam came racing into camp and knocked down a couple of lawn chairs in the process. The rest of us scattered like a covey of quail. The ram skittered up on top of the big boulder right by camp and put its horns down.

"I admire your greatness," Adam piped up. "And humbly beg your forgiveness for whatever faux pas I have committed in my sincere attempt to communicate in your tongue."

With another snort, the ram clattered off the boulder and walked downriver at a regal, leisurely pace. Troy was laughing. He looked relaxed, like his old laid-back self. Maybe, I thought, just maybe . . .

In the morning, as we were getting ready for the big hike, Troy told us he wasn't going. I had a feeling this was going to be the peak experience of the entire trip. Everybody, I think, was feeling the same way. No scary rapids to run, just a day in paradise to enjoy being together. I felt sure that a "senseless act of beauty" would do Troy a lot of good. I wondered if I was the reason he didn't want to go.

Rita pleaded with him—Pug, Star, Adam, too. I knew I couldn't. But Troy held out. "I just want to kick back," he said with a big smile. "It's too hot. Go have a good time. It's all right. It's what I want to do."

We started up the switchbacks behind camp that had

been cut to circumvent the impassible lower gorge of Tapeats Creek. I was last in line. I kept looking back over my shoulder at Troy, way down there by the boats. I was wondering if he was having another one of his headaches this morning. I thought about how alone he looked, about how many times he must have been left alone in his life, at boarding schools, at camp, with strangers while his parents were in Europe. No wonder he didn't want to go back alone to his place by the beach.

It was hot, so hot. It could have been a hundred and ten. The trail rejoined Tapeats Creek at last, and we plunged into an ice-cold pool. Hiking along the creek now, we could jump in whenever we dried off and started overheating. Pug and Star were hiking together up in the front, then Rita and Adam, jabbering away, and then came me, trailing a bit and all absorbed in my thoughts.

When we could see that the trail was going to leave the stream and switchback its way into the sky, we took a plunge in the last pool and had a long rest. A bright swallowtail butterfly passed through while we were there; so did a hummingbird. Just below the pool, on the edge of the fast water, the slate-gray bird we call the dipper back home was bobbing up and down on a mossy rock. I hoped it would swim underwater for us.

Adam pointed out some wild watercress, which we ate. "Not bad," Pug decided.

"Shall we?" Rita asked, eyeing the switchbacks above.

One last plunge in the pool, and then we attacked the scorching, oxygen-deprived, boulder-strewn climb.

" 'The steep and thorny way to heaven,' " Adam gasped, halfway up.

155

"Where's that from?" I managed. "I've heard it before."

"Willie the Shake. Shakespeare!"

During the last switchback, heaven indeed came into view, the most remarkable spectacle I'd ever laid eyes on. A quarter mile away, higher still than where we stood, Thunder River burst from twin caves in the cliffs and fell in streaming white torrents onto a layer of bedrock, and again into an oasis of cottonwoods. Everything the spray from the falls touched was blessed with greenery.

The five of us stood there panting and feeling absolutely on top of the world.

"That darn Troy," Rita muttered. "I knew he should've come."

Pug said, "I shoulda carried him up here."

Adam took a long drink from his water bottle. "He's missing the big enchilada, all right."

Star's interpretation: "His heart isn't right for it, yet."

A couple of minutes later, nearing the oasis, we were walking along a wide ledge under a tall cliff. Ten feet away from the trail, on a boulder perched above the abyss, an odd sight caught our eye. Someone had stacked rocks atop the boulder, three large, especially beautiful rocks that composed an elegant, gravity-defying vertical sculpture. I fancied the stones as a trio of acrobats dancing a vertical ballet, the bottommost member pirouetting on tiptoes. A wisp of wind, it seemed, or the slightest touch would send them tumbling.

Star was entranced. "Balance," she whispered.

Up the trail we flew, drawn to the big trees and the foot of the falls' final plunge. It was cool there, cooler still in the spray of the falls. Here we discovered another signature balancing act in stone, but on a smaller scale. "I love this," Star said.

"It doesn't take much to make her happy," Adam observed. "A few rocks, properly placed, will suffice."

About a minute later, Rita yelled, "Check this guy out." She was pointing straight into the sky, almost, at a skinny young guy with a ponytail. Somehow a hiker had climbed to the bedrock slope between the lower and upper falls. He had his head back and his arms out wide, as if he were about to lift off and fly.

Adam said, "There's our Druid, I betcha. The Stonehenge dude."

"Looks like a hippie to me," Pug said.

Of course Adam couldn't be content without trying to climb up there, too. And the rest of us, lacking sense and wanting to seize the moment, followed along. My personal excuse was overcoming my fear of heights.

"Nice place you got here," Adam told the rock artist as we approached along a seam that cut across the slickrock.

"La última," he replied with a wave to the grandeur spread out below. He had a wispy beard on his chin and a simple leather bootlace choker around his neck with two yellow-and-blue trade beads. His name, we soon learned, was Joe. He had a tattoo just above his ankle, a tattoo of a dancing turtle playing the tambourine.

Star asked, "Are you the Balancer?"

"That's my trademark," he replied. "Did you like them?"

All of us could see that Star was reaching for words wonderful enough. "They were . . . *beautiful*," she said finally.

157

"Why do you do it?" Pug wanted to know.

He stroked his chin. "I enjoy working with the forces of nature."

Adam was loving this. "What are they paying you out here for your line of work?"

"Deep satisfaction."

"Is that by the hour or by the job?"

"Definitely by the job. You can't count the hours. I find it relaxing and—pardon the pun—balancing."

I sneaked a glance at Star. He'd just said the magic word, and I could see it, like Cupid's arrow, landing directly in her heart.

Rita wasn't paying attention. "Are you here by yourself? What's the deal?"

"I'm making a circle route of the Four Corners states, counterclockwise. I started out at Window Rock, Arizona. I've been all through northern New Mexico and along the Continental Divide in southwestern Colorado, the canyonlands in Utah, and now I'm on my way to closing the circle at Window Rock this fall."

I asked, "You don't mean *hiking*, do you? Surely you're not doing all that on foot?"

"Hiking, sure. It's the only way to really see anything."

Rita had her hands on her hips. "So how long has this taken you?"

"A year and a half so far."

Pug asked, "You rich or something?"

The Balancer liked that one. He chuckled. "No, but I got some nuts and raisins, if you're hungry."

"Holy cow," Rita said. "This guy's too much. You got any shoes?"

He motioned up above. "I left 'em up by the cave."

"Wait a minute. You aren't telling us you've been higher than this."

"Sure. I've been inside the cave. Wanna see it?"

Twenty minutes later, to my chagrin, I was following our shoeless guide and the rest of our band into the darkness of the cave, with the river thundering below. With a glance behind, back toward the blinding sunlight, all I could see was water jetting into the sky and a pair of ravens tumbling past the mouth of the cave.

"Don't slip," I heard Rita say up in front of me.

"You do and you're into the history books," Adam answered cheerfully.

"There's a ledge here," I heard Joe call back. "It's not very wide, but it's wide enough. You have to let your eyes get adjusted to the light. There's more light than you think."

The farther I went, the more confidence I felt coming into my limbs. No twitching nerves, no sewing-machine leg, which is usually what happened to me over sheer exposure. Maybe it helped that it was so dark and I couldn't really see down. Strange to think I hadn't even known this Joe before, and yet I was trusting him with my life.

"Why are we doing this?" I asked, giddy with this first victory over a primal fear.

"Because we're crazy," Pug replied.

Chapter

21

Joe needed to cross the Colorado to begin the last leg of his circle trek. He told us he'd been hoping to hitch a ride with a raft party and have them drop him off down the river at Havasu Creek. He'd take a week hiking out the Havasu Creek trail, allowing plenty of time to hang around the waterfalls and visit the Supai Indian village.

From all sides, we told him, "Grab your backpack," "Love to have you," "Got plenty of food."

We felt tickled hiking back to camp with a new friend under our wing. Even Pug liked Shoeless Joe, as he'd dubbed him, which surprised me a little.

When we laid eyes on the Colorado again, from high above our camp, it looked different. A lot redder than before, yet it hadn't rained. I thought the river looked bigger and sounded louder as it rushed down Tapeats Creek Rapid.

But our boats were tied up to the tammies and Troy was down there on a lawn chair in the shade. Everything looked fine.

As we walked into camp, Pug made straight for Troy. "You shoulda seen it, buddy. It was unbelievable."

Troy said wearily, "There's a picture in the mile-by-mile."

Pug tried to rebound. "There was this cave where Thunder River shoots out of the cliff, and we all hiked back in there. Incredible, man, just incredible. This here's Shoeless Joe—he needs a ride down to Havasu Creek."

Troy's eyes went to Joe's feet. Joe was wearing hiking boots. Other than acting a little nonplussed, Troy didn't really acknowledge Joe even though he was standing right there.

I noticed Troy wasn't looking at me. He didn't want to look at me.

Adam was taking a long look at Troy as if studying a patient. Troy did look pale for someone so suntanned, and awfully fatigued for someone who'd sat in camp all day. On top of that, he was sweating profusely, which was new for him despite all the heat we'd been through. "Have you been having headaches?" Adam asked him.

"Buzz off, Adam. Save the doctor act for the girls."

"Seriously," Adam said, and put his hand to Troy's forehead. "You feel clammy, man."

Troy took Adam's hand away.

Adam persisted. "Any faintness? Muscle cramps? Have you been drinking lots of water? Cooling down in the river?"

Suddenly Rita was in Troy's face. "I told you, Troy. I've been tellin' you all the way down from Lee's Ferry."

"Back off," he warned her, and Rita stepped back.

"Step back, everybody," Pug ordered. "Give Troy some room."

With no trace of his usual jokes, Adam said to Troy, "I think you've got heat exhaustion. And heat exhaustion can lead to heatstroke real fast—if you don't drink a lot of fluids and get some salts into you right away, you're going to be in big trouble, my friend. Heatstroke can kill you. You collapse and an hour later you can be dead. Am I getting through to you? This is serious."

Troy considered it for a second, then waved him off. "I got some news that might be unhealthy for you guys, too. It's been a circus around here while you've been frolicking around with Clueless Joe or whatever this guy's name is. First, a helicopter comes by and drops a note—the river's going up to 92,000."

I gasped. That number sounded like the end of the world. What were Upset and Lava going to look like?

Everybody was reeling. Only Joe had no sense of what the number meant. He seemed more nervous about how Troy was acting than about the river.

"The water kept coming up . . . I kept having to retie the boats. All these groups kept coming by to get water out of the creek. It was a zoo around here. A rowed trip, three different motor trips . . . one of the motor guys told me that a lot of trips started getting canceled a couple days after we left Lee's Ferry—commercial and private. There aren't many people coming down behind us. So, if I have a headache, you might understand there's a reason. This whole trip is blown."

He finally looked at me. I couldn't tell if he was simply disgusted about everything or if he wanted to strangle me.

"Just leave me alone, okay?" he said, waving us all off.

Adam and Rita went for a walk way downstream along the rapid, while Star and Joe disappeared among the cottonwoods up Tapeats Creek. As Pug watched Star go, he looked a little lost, and I could understand. Even though he'd been slow at first to notice what was happening, he was getting the idea. He pulled up a chair alongside Troy.

I didn't have anywhere to go, so I hung out on my boat. I thought about trying out sleeping on the front deck tonight, like Kit did. It would be a lot cooler being over the water than anywhere onshore.

Troy and Pug were lounging in the kitchen area, with their backs to the river. This isn't doing Pug any good, I thought, whatever Troy's putting in his head.

I realized I should know what they were saying. Our safety might depend on it. Quietly, I stepped off the boat and sat at the base of the tammies where I could just barely hear what they were saying.

At first it was about the Bureau of Wreck-the-Nation. Troy was furious at them. Then they talked about Lava Falls, how big it was going to be. "So what's going to happen to us in Lava?" Pug asked.

"Simple," Troy said. "It's going to eat us alive."

"Can we portage it?"

"I asked two different boatmen. They said no. Cliffs on the right, some kind of springs and sawgrass on the left. They said don't even think about it—just get Lava over with."

After a silence, Pug said, "So how's it going with Jessie?"

163

Troy groaned. "It's a disaster. I don't know what she expects from me. Nothing I do is good enough for her."

"She's got an independent streak a mile long."

"That's one way of putting it."

"Save me from chicks like that," Pug was saying, like he was some big man of the world.

"No gratitude, that's for sure. But I've been doing a lot of thinking today, and I'm going to shake things up a little around here."

I strained to hear.

"Like what?" Pug asked. "What're you going to do?"

Troy just laughed. "Don't want to spoil it for you. You'll find out soon enough."

That was all I could take. Heart pounding, I crept back to my boat, grabbed a throw-cushion for a pillow, and lay down on the deck. I replayed how all of this had begun, back at Lee's Ferry. How wrong I'd been to go along under the circumstances. Of course it was going to end badly.

People stayed away a long time, waiting for Troy to cool down. By the time they came back, it was getting to be twilight. Star was incandescent, she was so taken with Joe. I could see Pug watching the two of them together. It was easy to see how happy Star was. Pug looked sick about it.

Joe was chopping vegetables for fajitas, Rita was barking out orders, Adam was getting his jokes rolling, and I was doing everything I could to stay busy, hoping for the best. Troy and Pug were still visiting quietly on their lawn chairs, watching the dark clouds that were beginning to build down the Canyon. Troy was taking a few

164

sips from a water bottle, but didn't look much better to me.

The wind was starting to blow the tammies around. It was coming from downriver, where the first bolt of lightning now appeared. Thunder came rumbling upriver. I recalled how quickly a Grand Canyon storm can come up.

We were running out of daylight, and running out of time before the storm was going to hit us. I got the lantern going. Everybody scattered to put up tents except Joe and Star, who both stayed in the kitchen. Joe said he had a little bivouac tent that didn't take any time to set up.

A bolt of lightning suddenly exploded with a searing snap not very far downstream. It took only about three seconds for the thunder to rumble upstream, more powerful even than the roar of Tapeats Creek Rapid.

The lantern ran out of gas, so we ate dinner by flashlights and lightning strobes as we eyed the pitch-black sky nervously. In the end the storm steered around us with only a few spatters of rain. It was so late nobody had the stamina to start boiling water and stay up to do dishes. We threw the dirty dishes in the bail bucket labeled SLOP and called it good.

"*Mañana,*" Adam declared.

The near-storm hadn't done much to cool us off; it had only contributed humidity to the heat. I told Star I was going to try out sleeping on the raft.

"On 92,000 c.f.s.?" she asked, wide-eyed. "You're going to sleep on the boat?"

"I've checked our knots, it's tied up tight. I figure it'll float the same as on lower water. I just want to try it."

Falling asleep at the end of a Grand Canyon day is never a problem. I was always so exhausted, it never took more than a couple of minutes. This time, with the monotonous rocking motion of the raft, it could have taken less.

It wasn't restful sleep. The repetitive motion of the raft kept me rowing in my dreams. I kept facing impossible situations—gigantic holes and standing waves, rocks and more rocks.

At one point the motion underlying my restless sleep changed, and it felt different through the layers of my subconscious. I felt choppy water, I felt current.

I lifted my head and looked around. It was the middle of the night. A little past full, the moon had cleared the rim and was lighting up the canyon walls and the surface of the river with ghostly clarity. Something was wrong, I realized. I was at least fifty feet offshore.

I looked again and saw Troy on the shore, holding the end of my bowline in his hands. He was standing there, just holding on to the end of the rope. What was he doing? My boat wasn't tied!

Wildly, I cast around to catch my bearings. My raft was on the margin between the eddy and the fast water at the brink of Tapeats Creek Rapid. Was he doing this on purpose? Was he about to let go of the rope?

I could jump on the oars if he let go, I told myself in desperation, but the raft would be swept down the right side of the rapid amid an impossible jumble of rocks and holes.

Where was my life jacket? Panicky, I started reaching around, trying to find it. It's on the shore, I realized, clipped to tammie branches. If he lets go, I'm dead.

Troy had a strange smirk on his face. He's doing this to scare me, I thought. He knew I'd wake up over the choppy water. He must be crazy! One good surge from the current and he won't be able to hold on. Doesn't he realize he could kill me?

"Troy!" I called out in desperation. My heart was hammering so hard it hurt. I was screaming now. "Troy!" All I could hear was the rapid.

Suddenly he was reeling me in. He brought me all the way in to shore. I realized that all I had on was my long nightshirt.

"Saved your life," he said with a grin.

"What were you doing, Troy? You nearly scared me to death!"

He smiled, and the smile acknowledged how much he'd enjoyed my terror and his moment at the controls of the power of life and death.

"I was retying your raft. I check on the boats every night, with the water coming up and all. Bet you never knew that."

"But what was I doing so far out there? I was fifty feet out in the river!"

He laughed. "Scouting the rapid?"

Chapter

22

"Not a good sign," Adam reported laconically as he sipped his coffee in the morning. He was looking down into the slop bucket. We went to see. A drowned mouse was floating above the greasy dishes, teeth up.

"That's disgusting," Rita said.

Joe picked the mouse up delicately by the tail and tossed it into the bushes. "Poor guy probably swam half the night before he cashed it in."

I thought, with a glance at Troy, I wouldn't have lasted but a minute or two in the river. I shuddered, picturing him stealthily untying my knots and then letting me drift out to the very edge.

Troy wasn't looking at me. He was eyeing the dancing turtle on Joe's ankle, with disapproval, I thought. Joe was barefoot again this morning. Something told me Troy didn't like Joe's ponytail, either.

Star wasn't saying anything, but I could tell from her expression exactly what she was thinking. The drowning of the mouse at our campsite, seemingly an insignificant event, was indeed a sign.

I would have argued that the death of the mouse was a preventable accident. But I wasn't in a mood for arguing philosophical points, or for arguing at all.

Yet arguing became the theme of the morning. It started as we were packing the rafts. We were tense looking at Tapeats Creek Rapid and the spot downstream where the river raged around the corner. The Colorado at 92,000 cubic feet per second was a beast on a broken leash. We were at Mile 132 and had ninety-three miles to go to reach the takeout at Diamond Creek, where a van with a trailer was going to meet us.

"Rig for bombs," I called tersely as I was checking all the tie-downs on the frame and the spare oars. "We got Upset to deal with today."

Adam wailed, "Now you've gone and got me all *upset*."

"Just don't upset the *Hired Gun*," Pug called. "We gotta keep our powder dry for Lava."

Joe had his backpack in his hands. "Which raft should this go on?"

Troy, who was pumping the tubes of his raft tight with his foot pump, looked up suddenly and said, "We need to have a meeting, everybody."

Rita was suspicious. "Whaddaya mean, a meeting?"

"A meeting," Troy repeated. "Jessie, Star . . . let's everybody get off the boats and sit down and have a little meeting."

Rita pursed her lips. "I don't like the sound of this, for some reason."

I was already holding my breath. What was this all about?

We sat in the sand and waited.

"Okay . . . ," Troy began. Suddenly he thought better of standing, and sat down among us, tucked in his long legs with slow deliberation, and continued. "I remember Canyon Magic saying these were not normal times. We're running at 92,000 c.f.s. now. Even the people who know this river blindfolded don't know what that means. We're way too loosey-goosey to keep approaching this the way we have been."

I thought, Where's he going with this?

I looked around. Pug was looking straight down into the ground. Adam was stroking his chin. Rita's black eyes were smoldering. Star had her eyes closed. Joe looked abashed and embarrassed.

"I learned something from Canyon Magic," Troy continued. "Even with five experienced guides, they had a trip leader. They don't split themselves apart all the time by voting. Everybody gives input, sure. But one person takes the responsibility. One person makes the calls."

Rita erupted. "So you've named yourself trip leader, Troy, is that what you're saying?"

He shrugged. "I figured you wouldn't be able to just listen, Rita."

"But you said at the beginning that everything was going to be democratic on this trip. Everybody remembers that, Troy."

"Well, so do I. But none of us could anticipate these conditions. I'm concerned about only one thing now: getting out of here. I don't want to think about maybe we'll do this and maybe we'll do that. I'm taking the responsibility because I already took it—I got the permit and rented all this stuff in the first place."

Rita shook her head emphatically. "That's not the way it was supposed to be. This is bait-and-switch, Troy. I told you I wasn't going to put up with this kind of stuff this time, and I meant it."

Troy raised his voice. "Settle down," he warned. "I know everybody wants to hike Havasu Creek. We'll take the time to do that one side-hike, that's all."

"What does Jessie think?" Rita demanded. "She's the other one rowing a boat. She's got a lot of responsibility, too."

I weighed carefully what I was going to say. Nothing that would set Troy off. I was scared for all of us. "I think this is sad," I said. "But we can't afford to fight about it—we have too much to lose. I thought we were doing okay making decisions by consensus."

I was surprised by who spoke up. Pug said, "We been doing pretty good when you think about it, Troy."

"Don't give up being democratic, Troy," Star pleaded. "Let's just keep trying."

Troy was shaking his head. "Let me give you an example, Star. Like yesterday, we could've lost the whole kitchen when the water came up so fast. Nobody was thinking about what could happen, like a trip leader would naturally do. I wasn't thinking about it, either. I just happened to be there."

"Got a point there," Pug said.

Troy stood up abruptly. "So that's it. I'm runnin' first, and I'll decide when we're going to stop for lunch and when we're going to camp and all that. We'll scout anything Jessie or I think should be scouted."

Rita gained her feet. "And you'll make yourself scarce when there's work to be done in camp."

171

He laughed. "Rita, don't act so put out. You're getting a free trip, or did you forget that?"

She turned to Adam as we were all getting up. "Adam, what do you think?"

Adam shrugged. "It's his bag of marbles, I guess. And the game wasn't all square when we got in."

"It just ain't fair," Rita muttered.

"Fairness is not an issue," Troy told her. "Oh, one more thing, everybody. With this 92,000 and all, we have to have our roles down on the boats. By now we pretty well know what to expect from each other in all sorts of situations. . . ."

I thought, What's he getting at now?

As Troy paused he glanced at Joe, and then he said, "I've decided we can't take Joe down to Havasu Creek."

"What?" Rita yelled. "What are you talking about?"

"That's twenty-four river miles, including Upset. Way too much responsibility, and it's illegal, too. He's not listed on the permit."

"Neither was Adam," I put in quickly. "That ranger could've busted us at Bass if he'd realized Adam was with us, not that motor group."

"I know that," Troy said wearily. "Adam's different. But adding this guy—it's illegal, and I'm not going to do it. He can wait for another group that'll take him."

"Hey, buddy . . . ," Pug pleaded.

"I can't believe this!" Rita exploded. "Troy's giving us this legal stuff. That's about as small as you can get. We got extra life jackets, we got plenty of food—"

172

"Get over it," Troy said regally, and turned toward his boat.

"I've had it!" Rita yelled. "Up till now I've been able to get along with you, Troy. I know nobody's perfect. I try to take people the way they are. But this is too much even for me. I'm not staying one minute longer on your boat!"

She sprang onto their raft and started undoing the straps across the tarp in the back. In a couple of seconds she had her hand on her dry bag. Troy jumped onto the boat, too, and yelled, "Leave everything right where it is!"

"You're like traveling with a two-year-old!" she screamed. "If you don't get your way, you just want to quit and go home. You're just a spoiled rich kid, Troy, that's all you are! You haven't changed at all!"

She stood up with her dry bag. The boat was rocking under her. "Nothing's ever good enough for you! If anything ever goes wrong, it's always someone else's fault! I've been sitting on this boat listening to you putting everybody else down, and I'm sick of it."

Troy moved to the middle of the tube to block her way off. "Put it back, Rita."

"For once in your life, Troy, try thinking about somebody else besides yourself. You think the world revolves around you—it's not all about *you*!"

Rita tried to force her way past him with her heavy dry bag. Troy didn't get out of the way completely. They were struggling over the dry bag; Rita lost her balance and fell headfirst, arms flailing, into the center of the raft.

Amid our cries and all the confusion, she struggled back up without taking the hand Troy offered. Troy retreated off the boat. Rita was looking at a bad scrape all the way down her right arm.

"Anything broken?" Adam worried.

"I don't think so," she said quietly.

Troy relented. "Okay, we'll take Clueless down to Havasu Creek." He said it in the way a military commander might, forced to change his mind. Troy's pride was mortally wounded, yet it was obvious he wasn't going to give an inch on having taken over as trip leader.

"Say you're sorry," Star suggested.

Troy glowered at her. "I'm not, okay?"

Suddenly Joe spoke up. "Thanks a lot, guys," he said, looking around to everybody. Then he added firmly, "I'll wait for another group."

Over our objections, he said, "You guys don't need four on a boat in this water."

Joe had his own standards, his own pride.

Star's eyes were about to brim over with tears. The only time I'd ever seen her cry was when she was moving into her new bedroom when she first came to live with me.

Joe told her, "Star, I've got all the time in the world to get across the river. It's okay. What do you say I look you up this fall in Boulder?"

"I'd like that very much," she said, and stopped the tears before they ran.

He kissed her on the cheek and withdrew his backpack to the shade of the first big cottonwood up Tapeats Creek.

Star offered to ride on Troy's boat so Rita could come

onto ours. Rita, who'd had her head down, looked up and said, "No, I want to stay where I've been. I don't want to split you up, and I'd miss the big guy too much. We're a team."

She gave Pug a smile to die for.

A few minutes later, we launched on our twelfth day on the river. Star stood up and waved to Joe; he waved back. Star sat down and I pulled to get into position to row Tapeats Creek Rapid.

Chapter

The walls drew in close as the middle gorge began to tail down into the river. The unleashed Colorado did not take kindly to being forced through Granite Narrows. The current line failed completely, and the boats were shunted unpredictably this way and that by the huge forces surging beneath us. Troy and I were both crashing into the walls, first on one side of the river and then the other.

Whirlpools appeared from nowhere, like tornadoes. Some of them sucked the tubes down so powerfully that the river came pouring in. I fought with all the strength I had. Troy was rowing like a man possessed, but I'm sure there was no joy in his heart. He'd taken the joy of the Canyon out of my heart as well. I hated him for what he'd done to all of us.

The gorge gave way ten minutes later and the river widened. Lighter shades of rock appeared, and we could see up and out again. On our right, Deer Creek Falls plummeted a hundred feet or more to the river through a crack in the sandstone. We surged by so quickly, it was out of view in a few moments.

The sky was turning dark on the left, real dark, and we heard distant thunder. I had a feeling this time it was going to get us. We raced downriver, putting the miles behind us as well as the rapids. Back when we were on 65,000 c.f.s., we'd calculated that we were going eight miles an hour. On 92,000, we could only guess. The walls were flying by.

Much sooner than I was ready for it, we were rounding the bend before Upset. We pulled out on the right, far upstream, to avoid being swept into the rapid without the chance to scout. Troy and I threaded our way through slabs of limestone to get down to where we could take a look at it. I was expecting the worst of the two holes at the bottom—the ones that I'd been trying to avoid all winter in my dreams. At this level I was expecting them to look something like a twin version of the hole in Crystal.

To my immense relief, the holes had lost their definition in the floodwater. Upset was going to be a huge ride, but it looked doable. "Let's hope for the same at Lava," Troy said.

I realized that the exact place we were standing was the farthest point I'd reached in October. A flood of memories threatened to overwhelm me, but I pushed them away. I had to focus.

Back at the boats, it was starting to spit rain. The sky was still black and blue to the south, high above the rim on the left side. Thunder kept rumbling like the end of the world was happening up there. Still, we were only getting spatters and wind.

177

"Let's go get wet," Troy proclaimed, and both boats pushed off. Nobody answered him.

I ran Upset bow-first, pushing on the oars, making little adjustments all the way through. Upset ran like an immense storm drain, dirty and fast. Below it, I looked back up at the staircase of whitewater I'd been rowing in my sleep all winter. Upset was behind me now. Strange to think I had actually just run it.

Of all the Big Drops, only Lava remained.

In the whirlpools at the bottom of Upset, Troy and I bumped boats. With a proud grin plastered across his face, he yelled, "Down to Havasu!"

Again nobody echoed his cheer. He'd succeeded in turning us to stone. Every mile we were seeing now was new for all of us, yet we were feeling no thrill of discovery, only a depressing combination of dread, regret, and shame. Seeing Havasu Creek with its blue-green pools, waterfalls, and hanging gardens was going to be joyless, nothing resembling our romp to Thunder River.

Troy, you kill the thing you love.

Between the raging current and the strange topography of the mouth of Havasu Canyon, it was tough managing a landing there. It wasn't a typical canyon mouth at all, just a narrow, unannounced slot around a corner on the left side. Fortunately we'd been hugging the left wall so we wouldn't miss it. A cluster of motor rigs appeared suddenly in a tiny eddy, and it was all we could do, rowing hard, to grab hold of those big rafts and put ropes on them. The back halves of our rafts remained out in the current that was racing toward the lip of the rapid, less than a hundred feet away.

We were disappointed to find that Havasu Creek,

world famous for its blue-green water, was running brick red. The rainstorm to the south was obviously affecting the drainage of Havasu Creek.

Nevertheless, we grabbed our daypacks, stuffed some lunch into them, and reached the shelves of stone along the shore by scrambling across the big rigs. Pug talked of raiding their beer, but it was only talk. We scrambled up the trail through layers of broken rock that led up to a shoulder and then back down to the creek.

The people from the motor rigs were all perched on ledges above the creek having lunch. They told us they'd tried to make this first crossing with the help of a rope, but their boatman said the creek was running too high and they'd have to skip the hike.

"Too bad," Troy said. He sounded happy about it. He turned to us and said, "Let's blast."

"Couldn't we just try it?" Star suggested. "We could all hold hands—maybe we could do it. This is our last hike together. . . ."

"Look around, Star. How much of a sign do you need? Even Mother Nature has it in for us."

It turned out we weren't even going to stop and eat lunch together. Troy was in a frenzy to get going. "Everybody's got something to eat in their daypacks," he ordered. "We can eat back on the river."

Troy and I reached the boats first, and were buckling our life jackets as the rest were climbing across the motor rigs and down into our boats. I had just taken a bite of an apple and was leaning down to tighten my sandals when I heard it—a roaring sound, sort of like thunder but different. I looked up, trying to determine where it was coming from.

Everybody was spooked: waiting, listening, looking around. Then we heard yelling up above, from onshore. We saw people running into view, all panicky. Somebody yelled down at us, "Flash flood!"

Before we could grasp that we were directly in harm's way, a torrent of red water came roaring out of Havasu Canyon's narrow mouth. The impact rocked the big motor rigs, and then a moment later it rocked us.

"Hang on!" I yelled, but I was too late. Rita was already flying out of Troy's boat into the river, without her life jacket.

Even though it happened fast, I saw it all. I was trying to keep my balance amid the brick-red violence of the water and the confusion of colliding rafts. I was looking directly at Troy. He saw Rita being swept away and he hesitated for half a second. Then, to my astonishment, he dove headlong into the river after her.

Our boats were rocking violently, threatening to flip with the force of the water blasting us from the side. The motor rigs were starting to ride over the tops of our tubes and we were about to be crushed. "Cut your rope!" I yelled to Pug as I pulled my knife from its scabbard on my life jacket and cut ours.

I was struggling to get control of the oars as we went over the lip of the rapid and bounced against the rocky shelves on the left. With a glance downstream, I saw that Troy had caught up to Rita and had hold of her in a cross-chest carry. He was buoying her faceup so she could breathe. The waves kept washing over them; they were visible only in snatches. "Don't take your eyes off them!" I yelled to Star and Adam.

I turned the stern downstream and rowed hard to get

180

to them. We caught up just below the tailwaves, in the boils. Adam hauled Rita aboard, gagging and choking, while Troy clung to the chicken line, coughing up water.

Adam made Rita keep her head down, between her knees, and Star held tight to her. Rita kept gagging. "Breathe, Rita," Adam said firmly. "Are you breathing okay?"

Rita couldn't talk yet, but she nodded emphatically. Adam reached for the back of Troy's life jacket and pulled him into the boat. Troy was exhausted. Star scrambled to the back of the raft to free the spare life jacket for Rita. With a glance upstream, I saw Pug strong-arming the oars, trying to keep the other raft off the wall.

Rita was sitting up now. Her color was coming back to normal. She was panting, hyperventilating, as if she'd never get enough air into her lungs again. Adam, smiling and shaking his head, turned his attention to Troy. "Great job!" he cried, slapping him on the back. "Good going, Troy—unbelievable!"

Rita took a long, hard look at Troy. She was trying to comprehend what had just happened. So was I. So, maybe, was Troy. We all knew what would have happened if she'd hit those monstrous whirlpools at the foot of the rapid before anyone got to her. Without a life jacket, she would have been pulled down in a second.

"You saved my life," Rita said. Her dark eyes stared at Troy with a mixture of gratitude and confusion. "You're a strange one, Troy, that's all I can say."

He shrugged it off with a smile, as if to say he'd take that for a compliment. His teeth were chattering. He didn't say anything at all.

There was no reason to go to shore. We bumped boats and transferred passengers midstream. Now that it was over, Rita was shaking, and not only from the shock of the cold water. She started digging through her bag, looking for warmer clothes.

"Let's get on down close to Lava," Troy said to me.

I nodded, spun my boat around, and pulled on the oars.

Chapter
24

We surged downstream toward Lava. The side canyons went flying by: Tuckup, National, Fern Glen, Stairway, Cove.

It was getting late in the day. We'd covered forty-five river miles since the morning. We kept looking for Vulcan's Anvil, the landmark that would prevent us from accidentally being swept over the edge of Lava. Pictured in the mile-by-mile guide, Vulcan's Anvil is the neck of an extinct volcano rising from the middle of the river.

Even before we saw the Anvil, signaling Lava more than a mile downstream, we could hear the River Thunder. Thunder on a scale even Crystal couldn't approach.

"Like the drums of doom," I heard Adam whisper.

We'd read in the guidebook that it was considered good luck to touch or kiss Vulcan's Anvil on the approach to Lava Falls. It was all I could do to keep control of the boat and keep it out of the whirlpools—we missed the opportunity. Keeping hard to the right, we searched the shore for anything that might serve as a camp. We found an approximation of one on tiny pockets of sand among boulders of dark basalt only a quarter mile above the falls. From the path leading downriver, we guessed our camp was actually a couple of wide spots on the scouting trail.

It was going to be a deafening evening. I told Rita she was excused from making dinner. *"Au contraire,"* she said. "And I give you fair warning, I'm feeling the need for some garlic therapy."

Troy was working on his raft, making sure everything was going to be tight for the morning.

He caught a glimpse of me coming down to his boat. He looked away.

"Permission to come aboard," I requested.

With a weary smile, he nodded.

I sat cross-legged on his deck; he was on his boatman's seat. I said, "I think I can wait until morning to take a look at Lava. How 'bout you?"

"Ditto."

"Well?" I asked.

"Well what?"

"What you did—diving into the river after Rita."

With a smile, he said, "Oh, that."

"Yeah, that."

"I can't exactly take credit for that. It happened so fast. I was shocked when I realized I was actually in the river."

"You're right that it happened fast. But first you looked around for a split second, and whatever you were thinking about, it wasn't about your own safety."

"I was trying to think what to do about the boat—we were tied up and getting blasted. But then I realized Rita just didn't have any time."

184

I hesitated, wondering if I should leave well enough alone. But it seemed like a moment that maybe wouldn't ever come again. "But why?" I pressed him. "I still don't understand *why* you did it."

"Just a reflex?" he said with a shrug.

"I don't think so. I saw your face. I think your reaction came from the best part of you—before all that thinking and calculating you're always doing."

He looked at me with those amazingly blue eyes, and for once I didn't feel like he was trying to use them to play me one way or the other. He said, "All those things Rita said about me this morning, about how I only look out for myself—she was just saying what everybody else thinks, anyway. That's the picture. That's the way it's always been for me."

"It's part of the picture, but not the whole picture, right?"

"I wish," he said softly. "I don't know, maybe I was just reacting to what Rita had said this morning. You know, trying to show she didn't know me as well as she thought."

I nodded encouragement. "I wish you'd give yourself a chance, Troy. You know, Star thinks everybody can create their own life, no matter where they're starting from."

He looked away, down the river. After a long silence, he said, "Where I'm starting from is not pretty, Jessie."

"You have to start somewhere," I said, touching his hand. "But you don't have to keep being your own worst enemy. You get your expectations up so high, Troy. Like for this trip, for us . . ."

He looked quickly back. "I can't help it. I just can't

help it. I always wreck everything. I bring people down and end up bringing myself down. I've never been able to stop myself."

"But you can."

"It's not that easy. This trip is a perfect example. I wanted this trip to be perfect, for you and for me. I tried so hard not to blow it. But I kept seeing the bad side of everything, right from the start. I just knew something would go wrong. Remember when you said you felt like I wanted you to flip? You were right—I did."

"But why?"

"When we first got on the river, I thought that if you kept having trouble, it would make you need me. I'd be able to help you, and we'd grow closer. But when you started getting so good at rowing, I could see that you *didn't* need me. So I started wanting you to fail. I wanted you to flip, especially in Crystal. That's what I mean—I get so angry and I don't know how to stop myself."

"If this is an apology, I accept it."

With that, he broke into his killer smile. "You know, I've never done anything before in my life like going in after Rita."

"Not many people have," I said, returning the smile.

He laughed. "That Rita! And to think I kept that wild woman's face above water without getting an ear bit off! I mean, she was just that close!"

The thought came to me that Troy was trying on a new image of himself, seeing himself in a new light. After what happened today, maybe he'd have something to build on, find a new place to start.

186

Suddenly serious, he said, "I won't see you again after this trip, Jessie. That's a promise. I'll leave you alone."

"What will you do?"

"I don't know yet, but I can see I'm going to have to 'get a life,' as they say. I've thought a little about computers, they sort of interest me . . ."

"Well, I wish you the best, Troy," I said. "You know I do."

He bathed me in those blue eyes. "I'll never forget you, babe. And I want you to have a glory run tomorrow in Lava, you hear me? I mean an out-and-out glory run."

"You too," I said. "And keep your sunny side up on the big river of life."

Chapter

25

Lava Falls. "The steepest navigable rapid in North America," the mile-by-mile guide calls it. John Wesley Powell, the explorer who first ran the river, was more than impressed. In his journal, he speculated on what Lava might have looked like eons ago. "What a conflict of water and fire there must have been here! Just imagine a river of molten rock, running down into a river of melted snow. What a seething and boiling of the waters; what clouds of steam rolled into the heavens!"

Troy and I hiked alone, before anyone else was up, to take a look. I hadn't been able to sleep and neither had he. In the cool of the dawn, we stood on the scouting escarpment at the brink of the rapid and took it in—the Power and the Glory.

I felt insignificant and frail in between the thousands and thousands of feet of cliffs towering above me, and the crushing force of the inconceivable amount of water plunging by below.

"Way to the ugly," Troy said.

I was already looking for a route. I saw right away

there was going to be no sneak of Lava Falls, no strip of safe water to be reached by scooting early off the enormous tongue. To the extreme left, there were gigantic pourovers that must normally be boulders high and dry above the river in the outwash fan of Prospect Creek. To the extreme right, it was absolute fury and chaos as the river was pushed against and over giant lava rocks.

"What do you see?" Troy asked.

"It's all pushing to the right," I said, "toward those monster waves at the bottom."

"Look at the weird ways they're breaking. Some moments it looks like you could go over the tops of them, like at Horn Creek. Other moments they're breaking back like Crystal. Are you thinking about doing your 'thing'?"

"I can't see how it could help here. What do you think about pushing in bow-first down the left side of the tongue?"

"And hope you don't get kicked into all the huge stuff down at the bottom. Same thing I'm thinking. Are you going to wear your lucky hat? The one Kit gave you?"

"Not a chance. I want to take that home with me! The hat's taking the ride in a rocket box."

"Too bad on the 10-scale they can only give it a 10."

We headed back to camp. Everyone was up and transcendentally cheerful. Rita was flipping pancakes. She was wearing a purple outfit we hadn't seen before. It looked sensational with her black hair. "Whatcha find?" she called as we came in. "What's making all that noise?"

"A Park Service recording?" Adam ventured. "Lava's all washed out, right?"

"Washed," Troy replied. "Piece of cake."

Adam asked, "Rita, are you going to make any predictions?"

"Heh-heh-heh," she laughed. "Kick its butt."

"Goin' to the boat-wash," Pug sang out.

Star's eyes lit up. "We'll wash ourselves clean in the river."

Adam leapt over and gave her a couple of those Hollywood-style air kisses, one on each cheek.

We kept moving the camp chores along. We intended to run as soon as other boats came. We'd all agreed that it would be more than foolhardy to try it without cover below. We were hoping for a motor rig or two.

That's what finally came down the river about eleven in the morning—two Grand Canyon battleships.

Now we had to hope that they would stop to scout, instead of motoring on through.

They pulled over. Their boatmen explained that the word was out about what had happened to the motor rigs in front of them, especially in Crystal. They weren't taking anything for granted. Yes, they'd be happy to cover for us. "How many flips you guys had?" one of their boatmen asked. "Just out of curiosity."

"Three," Troy answered.

"I'd say that's not too shabby."

Their thirty-five or forty passengers hiked up to the scouting rock with them, and all of us came along. I heard a lady asking Pug if we were going to go down Lava Falls in "those tiny little boats."

"Yes, ma'am. Should be exciting."

The boatman who'd asked about our flips, a man built like a fireplug, took us aside. "Have you guys heard about all the damage up at the dam?"

"What do you mean?" I asked.

"The river's been eating its way around the side of the dam through the cliffs. The concrete linings in the spillways are history, and word is, the river's been chewing up the sandstone like butter."

"So what's going to happen?" Troy asked him nervously.

"Well, the good news is, they say the water's finally coming down. They'll be able to close those spillway intakes."

"What a relief," I said. "It's so great to hear you say that."

Troy added, "Our takeout is tomorrow—we've been stressin' all the way down the river, not knowing what to expect."

"You aren't the only ones, I can tell you that. You know, this could have been a lot worse. For a while there, rumor had it that the boys at the dam almost lost their whole herd of horses—I'm talking about Lake Powell."

"Like how do you mean?" Troy asked.

"Talk was, the whole reservoir could've drained through the new routes the river was gouging out of the spillway tunnels."

I was only beginning to comprehend. "What would that have looked like?"

The boatman shrugged. "Your guess is as good as mine. I was picturing a wall of water coming at me high as a ten-story building. So I'm thinking that running

Lava at only 90,000—hey, we're getting away with murder!"

I managed a chuckle. "We'll try to look at it that way."

"We'll be waiting below. Don't worry, just enjoy it."

With that, the motor boatman turned and walked down the path toward his boats. Troy and I took our final scout. We knew it was going to be difficult or impossible to see where we were when we got out on the river. The rapid dropped so abruptly, there'd be no seeing over the edge until the last couple of seconds. We studied the riffle line coming off a boulder on river-left, which angled toward the brink at left-center. In the time that we'd have above the brink, we decided, we'd row as far as we could toward that riffle line, but not past it. If we reached it, we'd be set up for a ride down the left side of the tongue.

We walked back to the boats. It was so hot. I had Adam throw a bail bucket of water on me, and then I took a long drink. I snugged my vinyl gloves down on my fingers. My heart was pumping pure adrenaline.

The first motor rig started down the river. The man at the motor, the one who'd just confided in us, gave us a little salute. He drove the huge raft out to left-center, where we wanted to get to, and dropped out of sight. Their second raft followed about thirty seconds later.

We were alone again, but we knew they'd be covering us down below.

I looked over to Troy. He gave me a thumbs-up. "Good luck, Jessie," he said.

"Good luck, Troy. Good luck, you guys."

Troy said, "I want to run first just to get it over with. If it's okay with you."

"You got it," I told him. "Kit said it all happens in about twenty-five seconds."

Troy took about five deep breaths. Then he nodded to Rita to give a push and jump in the boat.

They were off. Troy was ferrying as hard as he could, to get as far toward our riffle line as possible. I gave him about thirty seconds, and then I nodded for Adam to push us off and jump in. "It's all yours, river lady," he said, crouching past me to get to his seat. "Have a good one!"

I started pulling hard, digging deep, rowing with my whole body. Pulling, pulling, pulling. With a glance over my shoulder, I saw Troy drifting toward the edge, possibly left of center. It didn't appear that he was going to make it as far left as we'd hoped. If he couldn't get that far over, I knew I couldn't.

With my peripheral vision I saw him disappear. I was still trying to get as far over as I could. Finally, midriver, I reached a place where it was useless to pull against the current. It was sweeping right, and we were on the verge of going over the brink, anyway. I pivoted the boat to face our bow downstream, and I let the current take us.

At last I could see. Just before we went over the edge, I could see that we were going to head down the right side of the tongue. It wasn't where I'd wanted to be. I saw that we were about to drop over a submerged ledge under the brink. It was going to have some snap to it. "Hang on!" I yelled as we went over the edge into the maw of the Thunder.

It was so steep, almost like we were in free fall. I braced for the snap and raised the oar blades high as we dropped into the ledge. I got thrown back by the jolt but held on to the oars and sat upright as we plunged on down the tongue toward the whitewater. As we hit the first whitewater, Star and Adam and the entire front of the boat disappeared in the deluge.

It was all exploding whitewater, towering whitewater, breaking from both sides. My oar blades caught the brunt of the turbulence and my arms flew forward as I instinctively tried to hang on to the oars. My arms would have been yanked from my shoulders if I'd hung on any longer, not that I could. The oars went flying out of control just as a wave from the right broke on me.

I felt myself leaving the raft over the tarped load at the stern. My right hand, clutching desperately behind me, found a strap. In the violence of the water, my body was awash and flying, but I hung on with that one hand. Thrown back down on the load, I found myself flipped onto my stomach.

My free hand found another strap. I'd ended up so far to the back of the raft, my lower legs were out in the river. I knew it was useless to try to climb back over the tarp and scramble for the oars. The boat was already brimful with water and would be impossible to row. If I stayed flat on my stomach, spread-eagled, I had a chance of staying aboard. It was like trying to hang on to the back of a sounding whale.

The bow was pointing directly downriver, as if I were still rowing. I saw it rise up and up onto the first of the mountainous waves in the lower right side of the rapid. Looming high above, its curling crest broke on us. I thought for certain we would flip, but we wallowed through, partly from luck and partly due to the ponderous weight of the water in the raft. I caught a glimpse of Star and Adam floating around in the front of the raft but hanging on with death grips.

We were deluged by torrents and more torrents. It felt like we were underwater, we were being pounded so heavily. Never had I even imagined whitewater on this scale. It was a force of nature all its own, it was a revelation.

Two, three more of these mountains of water broke on us. The last one swept Star out of the raft. She'd floated over the top of the tube, but she was still hanging on. Adam was struggling to resist being floated out himself while working his way over to Star. He managed to haul her back in.

It was only with Lava suddenly behind us and the boat spinning out of control in the whirlpools that I regained the oars. *"Bail!"* I yelled. With a glance downstream I saw Troy's boat right side up. They were screaming at the top of their lungs and so were we.

As soon as the motor rigs saw we were both upright, they took off. We fought for a mile or more to bail out the boats and get to shore. When we finally reached the shore and got the boats tied, we lost it. The six of us just outright lost it, screaming and hugging and falling down in the sand.

Chapter
26

We camped within sight of Diamond Peak, a dramatic desert Matterhorn. The heights of the Canyon here are drawn far back from the margins of the river, opening up the sky. The vegetation is sparse, the rock scaly.

We were camped at Mile 219, six miles short of the takeout, secure in the knowledge that we had survived. I sat by the river watching the first oranges and purples of the sunset reflect on all the dappled water pockets in a sand spit that reached far out into the river. The high water was finally on its way down.

Pug was lit by a sudden inspiration. He thought we should all climb to the flat-topped promontory high above our camp and watch the sunset from up there. We dropped what we were doing and scrambled up the spine of the slope. We panted for breath as we raced the advance of the sunset.

At a sort of collar under the cliffs of the promontory, we paused to recover from our climb before looking for a way up to the top. Most of us were bent over double and recharging our lungs. "Chuckwalla!" Adam cried.

"Chuckwalla yourself," Rita gasped.

"No, a lizard, a huge fat guy like a dinosaur."

"I gotta see this."

"He ran behind this slab."

We crouched and followed Adam under the slab, which had come to rest like a gigantic lean-to against the cliff. I took off my straw hat so I could see better. The only light in there was indirect; our eyes were taking a minute to adjust.

"Here he is." Adam was pointing into a crevice between smaller slabs of broken rock. "He's puffed himself up with air so you can't pull him out."

"Not sure I'd want to," Rita said. "He might take your finger off."

The huge brown lizard did have a prehistoric look to it.

"Look," Star said. *"Look."*

Star had found something else. In the deepest, lowest corner of the stone lean-to rested a large, perfect pottery jar. It had a delicate opening about three inches wide at its top.

"Left by the Ancient Ones," Star whispered. "Let's just admire it. It's a gift."

We all crowded in and crouched for a close-up look. It was colored a sort of burnished yellow, which was highlighted by the last rays of the sun sneaking through a fissure above us.

I noticed the expression on Troy's face. It wasn't one I'd ever seen there before. A simple shade of joy.

"This moment is a reflection of us," Star said. "Here we are, all of us, whole and intact."

"Rhaat onnn!" Pug agreed.

As we left the pot behind, I had the feeling that I'd be coming back to visit it again and again. I thought of my father. I wanted to take him through Crystal and Lava, take him to Thunder River, show him the Canyon, show him this pot.

We found a way up the back side of the cliff, onto the top of the promontory. The sun, spoking shafts of light and color all across the Canyon, had waited for us to enjoy this last burst of splendor together. We were drawn immediately toward the edge, where we'd be able to look down on the river.

There was our camp, far below. The *Canyon Wren* and the *Hired Gun* were rocking side by side in the eddy.

Without anyone's having suggested it, we were forming a circle, holding on to each other. We laughed, and we cried, knowing that our time together was coming to a close.

Behind us now, the redwall of Marble Canyon, the turquoise waters of the River of Blue, the bristling drama of the dark Inner Gorge. Behind us, the cottonwood-lined climb to the stream that bursts from the depths of the earth and into the sky.

All our rapids were run, one hundred and sixty of them. The roar of the River Thunder was receding into memory.

Below us, the Colorado swept by in silent majesty.

I was leaving the river knowing myself better than ever before. Perhaps that was the river's gift to each of us. How can rock and light and moving water do this? That's a mystery I could take a lifetime to explore.

Author's Note

In writing *River Thunder* I've drawn heavily on my own experiences in the Grand Canyon, as I did in my earlier novel, *Downriver*. So far I've been fortunate enough to row my own raft down the Colorado River through the Grand Canyon ten times. My wife, Jean, and I usually put these trips together ourselves, traveling with only a few rafts and a group of four to eight friends. Once we did the trip solo, just the two of us with our one raft.

For this story, I was attempting to recapture, in Jessie's voice, the emotional quality of rowing the Canyon for the first time, as well as to re-create the conditions I'd encountered on my own first trip. Little did Jean and I know back in the summer of 1983, as we prepared for that first trip, that we were going to be involved in what would become a legendary event in the history of river running in the Grand Canyon—the high water of 1983, often referred to among longtime Grand Canyon boatmen as The Flood.

For the first time since the completion of Glen Canyon Dam in 1963, the reservoir behind the dam, Lake Powell, was virtually filled to the brim. A catastrophic miscalculation of the winter snowpack and the spring runoff had resulted in more water's coming into the reservoir than anticipated, and at a much faster rate. It became necessary to release water past the dam and into the Grand Canyon at levels no one had seen since the pre-dam era—all the way up to 92,000 cubic feet per second.

Rafters on the river at that time had no idea how serious the emergency at the dam really was. The massive spillway tunnels that skirt the dam on either side were being put to use for the first time, and the concrete linings of the tunnels failed. The spillways began to run red as the rushing water carved immense cavities inside the cliffs. The Colorado River was threatening to find a route around the dam. It would cost more than thirty million dollars in the wake of this disaster to redesign the spillways and repair the damage. It had been a close call.

It was a heady time for rafters, private and professional alike, who happened to be on the river. Helicopters were flying up and down the Canyon, dropping messages on unsuspecting boaters, warning them about the rising water and advising them to seek higher ground. Thirty-seven-foot motor rigs were flipping in rapids like Nankoweap that normally posed no threat. Smaller rafts, highly maneuverable, almost seemed to have the advantage. The dory speed run described in *River Thunder* is based very closely on the legendary run completed at that time that set a new rowing record for the Canyon: 36 hours, 38 minutes, and 29 seconds.

On our '83 trip, I was rowing a fifteen-foot raft, often

through waves more than twenty feet high. On the day of our launch, the river was running 65,000 cubic feet per second. Our rafts were rowed by four men and one woman, only two of whom had rowed the Canyon before. We managed to complete the trip with only two flips among us, a result that gave me confidence that Jessie and Troy's combined total of three flips in the novel was realistic.

Running the Colorado River through the Grand Canyon is sometimes called the great American adventure. I hope that my depictions of the magic of moving water and life on the river will encourage readers to discover this adventure for themselves. River companies like my fictitious Canyon Magic take more than ten thousand people a year through the Canyon, and do it with a remarkable safety record. My mother went on a motorized trip with a professional company when she was seventy-three years old, and had the time of her life.

About the Author

Will Hobbs is the author of many award-winning novels for young adults, including *Downriver*, the companion to *River Thunder*. A graduate of Stanford University, he grew up in Alaska, Texas, and California. Will loves hiking and running rivers and has rowed his own whitewater raft down the Colorado through the Grand Canyon many times. He lives in the mountains outside Durango, Colorado, with his wife, Jean.

Turn the page for more thrilling adventure
in the companion novel *Downriver*.

Winner of the California Young Reader Medal and
the Colorado Blue Spruce Book Award

"Exquisitely plotted, with nail biting suspense and excitement." —*School Library Journal*

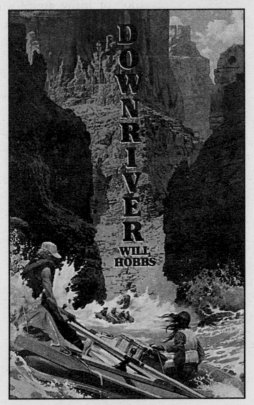

0-440-22673-2

On sale now from Laurel-Leaf Books

◇ **‖** ◇

I STUMBLED ON A ROCK THAT WAS BARELY sticking up, my legs were that tired. Flailing for balance, with the pack working against me, I slipped in the mud and almost went down. I still couldn't believe this was really happening. I couldn't believe my dad had done this to me.

For five days Al had been leading us into the most rugged corners of the San Juan Mountains in southwestern Colorado, coaxing and pushing us over the passes and into the peaks, through good weather and bad weather, mostly through bone-freezing rain and sleet. "October in the mountains," Al said with a grin. "You live a whole lot closer to the edge."

The going was always either straight up or straight down—we rarely followed trails. There were eight of us, four guys and four girls including me, all serving nine weeks in this outdoor education school from hell. Al called his program Discovery Unlimited, but we called it Hoods in the Woods, the name we inherited from the previous waves of misfits who'd come through the place.

Al kept us marching all day under heavy packs, grinding us down in preparation for . . . for what? He would never say when you asked him. He'd only reply with a wink or a knowing grin. Hike, freeze, starve, break out the ropes and carabiners and risk your life every day—for what?

"Just a mile till camp, guys," Al said. "Think about a sunny day."

I couldn't. I could see nothing but the frightening dark tunnel that was my future. I saw no images there, no hopes, only blackness. All my happy images lay in the past, all the happy scenes with my dad when it was just the two of us. I tried to dwell on the good times as I walked, but those pictures, those voices, only intensified my feeling of loss and left me staring once again into that black tunnel.

"How's it going?" Suddenly Troy was walking at my side.

"Okay, I guess."

"You don't look so happy."

"I'm ready to be in camp. When Al says a mile, you know it's two or three."

"It's part of his charm."

We jumped a little creek and started up a steep slope. Soon neither of us had enough breath to speak, but thinking about Troy took my mind off me. He seemed much older than the rest of us, just from the way he carried himself. It was like he was sizing up this whole situation from the outside. I'd been wondering if he was going to be friendly, and now it seemed he was.

Camp at last. I found a dry spot under a tree and eased

my back against its trunk. Troy sought me out and sat cross-legged, up close. "Does the climbing scare you, Jessie?" He was looking at me with the calmest and clearest blue eyes I'd ever seen.

"Yes," I allowed, looking away.

"I thought so." He said it knowingly, in a way that promised help. When I looked back to his eyes, they kind of locked on to mine and wouldn't let go. Apparently he never needed to blink, and he wasn't going to look away. His eyes seemed to be challenging me to . . . to what?

"I'm doing okay so far. . . ."

His eyes let me go. For now, I thought. I was fascinated by him. Someone was yelling that he was supposed to be one of the cooks. Troy reluctantly unwound his long legs and said, "Catch ya later."

We drew in close to the campfire that night, putting off as always the moment when we'd have to get into our freezing bags and face the shivering hours of the night. We knew Al would make his speech about the next day and of course he did, as he poked the fire. "We've got the climbing skills down now, guys—it's time for a true test. After that we'll head back to base camp for hot showers, real food, and our beds."

I pictured the little log cabin that I shared with Star, and how good it would be to stoke the potbellied stove until the stovepipe turned red. So what was this big test going to be?

"Tomorrow," Al announced, "you're going to climb Storm King Peak, elevation thirteen thousand, seven hundred, fifty-two feet. And it's no puppy. You'll know you've accomplished something. We'll draw straws this evening for climbing partners. Troy, you're going to be the navigator—you haven't led yet."

"Nothin' against Troy," Rita said in her nasal, right-at-you New York accent, "but if this Storm King is such a big deal, why not let Freddy lead? We know *he's* good at it."

I glanced over at Freddy. The campfire light flickering on his deep brown skin, black eyes, and shaggy black hair revealed, as usual, nothing in the way of response. True, I thought, he's capable, but he's practically mute. I'd much rather follow Troy. I had reason to believe that Troy cared whether I lived or died.

Al was shaking his head emphatically as he spread the topographic map out on the ground. "Troy will do just fine. He's your leader for the climb. Star, you're shivering—come into the light and warm yourself up. Folks, everybody needs to develop these skills, every one of you. Sometimes there isn't going to be anybody else around."

"But we travel in a pack," Adam pointed out with his trademark mischievous grin. Our redhead loved nothing better than sidetracking a conversation. "So whoever's going to lead can study the map and the rest of us followers can go to bed."

"Seconded," said Pug, the Big Fella, stretching one giant leg out toward the fire and nudging a piece of wood into its center.

Al scratched behind an ear, amid the wiry gray hair that stuck out beneath his wool cap. He was rocking slightly on his haunches; he preferred to squat rather than pull up a log or a rock. He reminded me in his body language of an aborigine or a tribesman from the Amazon, right out of one of the slide shows my dad used in his anthropology classes. "Sometimes," Al said slowly, "sometimes self-reliance is the key to survival, but other times cooperation is. Let's everybody study this map, and then tomorrow, on the mountain, we'll pool our knowledge. Whenever somebody's wondering if you're doing the right thing, bring it up with Troy."

"What if the right thing, the way we figure it, would be to go into Silverton for burgers?" suggested Adam.

Everyone had a smile or a laugh, including Al. With Adam, there was never anything at stake. He was so easy.

I could sense Heather getting ready to object, and I braced myself for her voice, which I found jarring and oddly mismatched with her broad shoulders. When she thought something was unfair, which was most of the time, her voice rose even higher than its usual pitch and her speech came out squeaking and gasping, because she couldn't talk and breathe at the same time when she was upset. "What I don't get is, we can all cooperate on the climb, right, except for you, Al. You won't help us at all, right?"

"That's what this is all about, Heather—you guys have the skills now. You make the decisions, you make the choices, you live by the consequences. You'll be on your own. I'll just tag along for the scenery."

Troy, I noticed, was attending to all this. Watching, listening, but withholding comment. Everybody was looking to him, including Al. Troy was a heavy, and everybody knew it. We were all wondering when he'd take Al on, but he was holding back.

When Heather saw that Troy wasn't going to respond, she said in that voice like an abused violin string, "You say we get to make the decisions, but really we're just puppets, and you're manipulating us. I don't like your rules, Al. I can't accept that you get to make them all up. Who gave you that right?"

That's telling him, I thought. That's exactly how I feel. This guy reminds me of my dad.

"Right on, sister!" thundered Pug, who was only half-listening, his attention focused as usual on his biceps. Despite the cold, he was wearing a T-shirt cut off at the shoulders, and was admiring the firelight's reflection on his muscles. Without thinking about it, he proceeded to punch Troy playfully in the arm. Maybe it was Pug's way of showing gratitude to his buddy for bestowing his nickname, the Big Fella.

"Why don't you blow your whistle, Heather?" suggested Adam with his wide ironic grin. "Blow your whistle, loud and clear."

When you blew your whistle it meant you wanted out, it meant you were going home. I'd been wondering all week when somebody was going to do it. I'd sure thought about it, about getting out of this place. But I figured out why I hadn't done it: aside from not wanting to be first, I would have had to face what I'd be going back to. Was there "home" back there for any of us?

I could only answer for myself. As for the others, their lives were mysteries. We were as far apart as galaxies in the night sky. Star and I shared a cabin back at base camp, yet I had little sense of what kept her going. She seemed so frail, I'd have guessed she'd be the first to blow her whistle. If the last week had been torture for me, what must it have been for her?

· 2 ·

THE NIGHT BEFORE STORM KING, I GOT NO
rest. I was whirling and tumbling inside the car with the
world spinning out of control all around. I woke up and
took a drink from the water bottle between Star and me.
It was pitch dark, still the middle of the night. When I got
back to sleep, I was climbing a mountain with Troy and
some people who weren't even in our group. I kept saying
that we should turn back, we were late for something, but
Troy wouldn't. Then I slipped, and was hanging from his
grasp for the longest time, but then he let go and I was
falling, falling, falling.

Thrashing around in the tent, I woke Star. "Are you
okay?" she was asking.

"I'm okay," I said, barely coming to. "Just fell off a
mountain, that's all."

"That's not good, Jessie."

"Well I guess not, seeing as how we're going to be

climbing a peak with ropes and all that stuff in a few hours."

"Imaging can make things happen," she whispered. "You have to work on your images."

"It's not like I can control my dreams, Star. I've had falling dreams since I was little."

What I didn't tell her was, they started right after my mother died. I'd told her enough.

Unable to get back to sleep, I lay shivering, and wondering if my dad had any idea that I still get those dreams. I told myself that the nightmare had nothing at all to do with actually falling, or with mountain climbing. Skiing doesn't scare me, flying doesn't either. Mountain climbing, I told myself, I can do that if I have to. If *Star,* for crying out loud, if Star can do it, then I can too.

At breakfast I drew Freddy for my climbing partner. I was relieved. As withdrawn as he was, he wasn't an exciting companion, but he was a capable climber, probably the best among us.

The eight of us, with Al trailing, set out from the trees at dawn, trying to make as much time as we could before the weather turned bad, which it tended to do every day around noon. Troy, our navigator for the day, led the way, along with Heather, his climbing partner.

When we cleared the trees, we couldn't see the peak. A high ridge, serrated and imposing, blocked our view. Troy started up the ridge, making good time. He didn't stop to look at his map and he didn't ask anyone for a second opinion. I wondered if we should be "conferencing," the way Al wanted us to, but like Troy, I was anxious to get on with it before the weather turned bad. Already the clouds were boiling up out of the blue skies.

I walked three steps behind Freddy. I felt awkward with him. Freddy was not exactly an artist when it came to conversation. Anyway he seemed content to ignore me. I had the feeling he was something of a wildman, and I was a little afraid of him, like maybe he had a violent streak and had committed some awful crime. He was the only guy, I noticed, that the Big Fella wouldn't wrestle with and sit on whenever he wanted to play or show dominance or whatever it was. Freddy had some kind of signal that said "Don't touch," and even Pug, the sensitive soul that he was, could pick up on it.

Freddy slowed a bit, and I thought for a moment that he wasn't sure if we were going the right way, but he said nothing. I stopped and caught my breath. Freddy sniffed the wind, like an animal. He did that often. His jet-black eyes would focus, never on the people, but on the clouds and the peaks, on little gray birds flitting around, on rocks and dirt and trickling water. Someone said Freddy was from New Mexico. When Freddy did speak, it was in a musical Spanish accent. Like Pug, he never flirted with the girls, but unlike Pug, he didn't joke around with the guys either. Freddy was a loner.

As I caught my breath, I watched Troy's bright shock of blond hair bobbing as he chattered with Heather. I wondered what they were talking about.

I was enjoying the walking, happy to have left my enormous backpack in the trees and feeling weightless by comparison, with only my daypack on my back, even if the slope was getting steep and the air thinning by the moment. We were somewhere around thirteen thousand feet, heading for close to fourteen. Al bounded alongside us, appearing out of nowhere with a huge grin plastered across his face and a cheerful "Great day, isn't it!" He wasn't even breathing hard. He's in his mid-forties, like my dad, and strong and lean as a whip. Even his gray hair is like that, I thought, springing out like steel wool from under his cap and jumping out of his nostrils and ears. There were moments when you almost wondered if you liked him, but those were the rare moments he wasn't killing you, and they passed quickly.

"Say, look at this," Al said, and swooped to pick up a bit of bone, something I would never have had the energy to notice while climbing at thirteen thousand feet. "Power object!" he proclaimed.

Freddy, looking vaguely interested, slowed up as Al held it out for us to look at. "Bird bone—hollow. What do you think, Jessie? You're a Colorado girl, from Boulder and all."

"I'm too winded to even speak," I managed. "How am I going to think?"

"Freddy?"

My climbing partner shrugged.

"Maybe a bit of Mr. Raven's wing, chewed by Mr. Coyote," Al theorized. He kept looking at Freddy as if Freddy should really know. Then he took the leather pouch that hung from around his neck, opened it, and dropped the bone fragment in among the rest of his "power objects," whatever they might be. I could never tell if Al was as weird as he sounded, but I guessed that he was. He was always grinning. I had my own images of Vietnam vets, maybe from seeing too many movies, but I knew I didn't trust him. I didn't buy his premise that taking kids out in the mountains and making them suffer will fix what ails them. And to live the way he did, year in and year out, he had to be a madman. I sure wasn't going to respect him for it. So I was always off balance with him.

I looked around for Star and Adam, but they were well behind. Adam would have milked some comedy out of the "power object."

It wasn't time for fun, it was time for technical climbing. We'd run out of walkable ground. Al dropped back to take up the rear on our "true test" and leave us to our own devices. As Freddy took his coil of rope off his shoulder, Troy waved us around him and Heather. The clouds were turning dark and the wind was suddenly blowing hard. I could see the uncertainty in Heather's body language even though she avoided my eyes. Words rarely failed her, but on this occasion she didn't say anything. Her partner motioned toward the face of the looming peak and said, "You lead, Freddy. Find us a route."

I watched Troy as he said it. It was a tough admission for him. He was such a natural leader and such an able person physically. It was a defeat, having led all the way from camp, to have to follow now. I glanced to Freddy, to see how he would take it. He shrugged.

We broke out our nylon climbing harnesses and rigged them snug. Mine dug into my crotch a little. I hated it. I thought about how my father had never done any technical climbing in his life and yet had blithely shipped me off to Hoods in the Woods, knowing that climbing was a lot of what they did. Carefully I secured the rope to my harness. "Check my knot for me, would you, Freddy?"

He looked me all over. "Okay," he grunted.

Frightened, I adjusted my helmet with the strap under

my chin, and looked to Troy for reassurance. My fear had boiled up out of nowhere like the clouds, and I could taste it. Troy's eyes skittered away for once. He bent over and busied himself getting his rain gear and his helmet out of his daypack.

"Oh well," I thought, "here goes nothing." I can't believe that was my attitude, given my fear and my nightmares, but I'd always liked to push myself. Driving too fast, that goes without saying. Wanting to hang out with older guys. I'd wear all white, I'd wear all black, I'd wear my hair long, cut it off short, put a purple streak in it just for fun. I wasn't afraid of what people would think. My dad liked to say it was a natural stage that he had gone through too. "Young people tend to see everything in extremes, not only in our society and not just in modern times—they always did." Anthropologists talk like that. He's studied cultures all over the world, but mostly in books. He hasn't done any field work in his beloved Amazon since my mother died.

"You think in extremes, Jessie," he liked to tell me. "Everything's either wonderful or it's 'blown.' "

Freddy led the way, climbing easily if not gracefully, pausing here and there to hammer pitons into the rock. His stocky body seemed to hug the earth naturally. I'm Freddy's height, but I'm hollow-boned like Al's raven and naturally defiant of gravity. I have a long-distance runner's stride, I've always been able to leap and jump, and I've always liked skiing because it set me free, left me attached only marginally to the ground. Now as we started across the face of this peak, the depths were pulling powerfully at me from below, and I felt my strengths turning to weaknesses.

"Don't look down," Freddy cautioned from above me.

His warning came too late. That's exactly what I'd just done, glanced at the drop. It had to be a thousand feet. I'd seen the sharp boulders jutting at crazy angles at the bottom of Storm King Peak's north face, and they seemed to be rushing up to meet me.

"Jessie, don't look down."

Too late. My stomach was in free-fall already, and I was so dizzy I thought I might black out. Suddenly lightning broke from the blue-black sky and thunder exploded almost instantaneously, with all the force of a sonic boom.

I was aware of gasps and swearing from the rest of them. I knew I hadn't been hit by the lightning, but all the same the sheer terror of the moment chased the strength from every fiber in me, and I was paralyzed.

I glanced up. There was Freddy, with his shaggy black hair blowing in the wind, his face all lit up with a feral sort of joy born of the wild moment. Whoever he was, my life was now tied to his, and our eyes were locked together. He said, "You can do it, Jessie. Move your right foot to that little spot over there, and your right hand to that finger hold."

"I can't," I whimpered.

From behind me and below I heard Rita, the self-proclaimed Thief of Brooklyn, holler the loudest stage whisper I'd heard in my life. "Jessie's got that 'sewing machine leg' Al talked about."

It was true. I was so afraid, the nerves in my right leg were buzzing and the leg was twitching up and down.

"Take a few deep breaths," encouraged Al. I glanced down and back toward the ridge, and saw an impression of his face, wide-eyed under his helmet.

"Look at that leg shake!" I heard Pug yell from below. He obviously loved the spectacle of the jumping leg but had no idea it was connected to my feelings.

"Pug," Freddy called down, "keep your mouth shut."

Pug yelled something back at Freddy. I could feel the spasms in my leg—I didn't need to look. What was worse, numbness was spreading through the rest of my body.

"Everyone cool it except Freddy," ruled Al. "He's her climbing partner." I looked back and below, the way I had come, looking for Troy. He was the only one I could trust. I was hugely relieved to see him appear behind Pug and Star. "Troy . . . ," I said desperately, "I'm in trouble. Help me!"